BOOK 5 OF THE SANCTUARY CHRONICLES

# THE WALL

# GREG RODE

ISBN: 978-1-957723-76-1

Rode. Greg
The Wall

Edited by: Melissa Long
Illustrations by: Merissa Jones

Published by Warren Publishing
Charlotte, NC
www.warrenpublishing.net
Printed in the United States

A very long time ago, I was looking for
something new to read and asked the smartest
guy I knew about a particular book in his
collection. "That's an important book," he told
me. The idea that a book could be important
instead of just schoolwork got my attention.
He was right too; it was an important book.
These many years later, having read that book
and hundreds of others, as well as writing
a handful, I think they all are in their own
way. Whether they teach you something;
make you laugh, cry, turn more lights on;
or take you away from the burdens of life
for a few hours, there is a little bit of
magic in all of them from start to finish.

This one's for you, Dad.

Don't miss
*The Sanctuary Chronicles*
by Greg Rode:

# CHAPTER 1

"Life, liberty, and the pursuit of happiness." I had a dark-blue T-shirt back in the day which displayed that phrase proudly around an American flag tucked into a circle. It's a pretty simple list of ideals, and my group has all three of those things hidden up here in New York's Catskill Mountains, finally free of the infestation of zombies and other malcontents that had survived the end of the world. Well, not the end of the world exactly since some of us are still here, though a good shitload fewer. Some would say the end of the world as it was, this scouring of the earth in blood, stunning violence, screams, suffering, fear, and ultimately survival of the fittest—or the damn lucky or lucky damned—is overdue. Those might be from the crowd that looks to a certain large black book for guidance or might be from the practical bunch who think we're skidding wildly on an icy river toward a frozen waterfall that drops into an endless abyss of selfish behavior, tiresome consumption, and never-ending search for the "next big thing" while overlooking all the amazing things that are right here, right now.

Like Eve slumbering next to me after a good night's sleep. A darn amazing thing. We're in one of the cabins on the property that has been in my family for over a century as something of a summer vacation getaway, now providing our small group with sanctuary. After meeting Eve more than two years ago, as the first person delivered to me by a small army of zombies led by a zombie queen of sorts, or what we now call "alphas"—a little smarter, more powerful, and "cleaner" than the others—I've been cautiously mooning over her.

Not "mooning" like pulling your pants down. Well, I guess pulling my pants down eventually has been in the back of my mind at times.

I'm a little all over the place this fine morning.

After those years, many adventures, and losing Eve for a short while along the way, she came into my room last night, and we slept together. As in the same bed, not the other way. There's no rush for that now. It's good to wait for things you want. You know, the pursuit of happiness.

Listening to her breathe, mingled with the early morning sounds from the great outdoors coming to life through the screen door, brings me peace, which is no small thing to underappreciate these days. We've been through a lot, our group, and some have regrettably come and gone as our story has made its way across time. Some have happily gone … well, they might not have been happy about it, but the rest of us are happy they're gone, so it's all about perspective.

If this were a book, the author would probably spend a number of pages telling the reader about everything that has happened to date, especially if it's a series of books, which could take a while. I let my mind drift in the hazy level of consciousness just after waking and think about what I'd say if I were writing "our" book. Tell all of the history? The stories of the dead? No, not this morning; I'm not in the mood for mourning. Tell about who is still alive and kicking? Seems to make sense.

Aside from Eve and me, there's Morgan, Kuniko, Maya, Bob, Amy, and our two dogs, Ajax (badass Rottweiler) and Jack (badass German shepherd). I guess we're all badasses to some degree or other, too, since we're still alive—check the box for "Life." Morgan is my sister. She'd been living out in Colorado when the bulk of the human race stopped racing and started dying, and eventually made her way here to see if I was still alive. Amy is a young teenager Eve met during her side trip in Pennsylvania before bringing her here, and Kuniko, Maya, and Bob are three people we recently just rescued from a house of horrors Morgan had discovered on her trip across the country. We tried to save more than just the three of them, but a horde of zombies and a few asshole humans got in the way of that. Not all the people still alive are in the "good guy" category, but at least that batch isn't a problem for us anymore.

Just a few weeks back, the remnants of the army paid us a visit, told us everything had been premeditated to give our country something of a do-over, offered to let us join them in camps that are being built to get going on the doing-over, but we declined. Hanging out with people who have big guns, walls, and other neat stuff like tanks and bazookas is probably a good plan nowadays, but large groups are also much more noticeable targets for the monsters. And there's the small thing about them telling us they killed almost every human being on the planet *on purpose*. And not just killing, like with bombs that had ended things instantly for most, but slaughter, painful slaughter, at the hands of the army of the damned of their own creation. While their offer had been put forth without strings attached, I was confident they weren't telling us everything, and "Come hang out with us" was never going to be as straightforward as they'd tried to sell it. Thanks, but no thanks, we said. Surprisingly, they left us alone and trundled off down the road, and we've had near silence, peace, and solitude since then. And there is the check for "Liberty." So, for the most part, we're all good.

If this were a book, that last couple of sentences would mean it was all about to change, and books being what they are, the change wouldn't necessarily be for the better.

# CHAPTER 2

Like most of my life, I don't exactly have a plan. But really, who does?

Other than fairly intangible ones, like "have a career" or "retire as soon as I can," I didn't have specific plans back in the day. Oh, I think ahead all the time but not, like, *way* ahead. Maybe it's more about not having a "plan." Thinking ahead has kept most of us breathing along the way, but now that we're settled here at the cabins and have a larger-than-before group, no remaining zombies in the area, plentiful food in the vacant grocery stores of the nearby towns and on the farms sprawling like organized quilts across the hills down in the valley, a happy place to stay since many of my childhood memories are tied to it, I haven't really thought beyond the basics of food, shelter, and survival. Will I (we) just stay here and eventually die of old age? Will our little lakeside colony grow with more people either emigrating here and/or maybe having children? Can the humans ultimately win and start over for real? That latter scenario seems the most unlikely since there were millions of monsters at the beginning of the end, according to the army guys, so I assume there are still a shit-ton left—or however one would handle zombie counting—and not many people remaining to kill them, despite the confidence of the visiting colonel and his troops.

Speaking of them, now thinking back to our conversation, the colonel said they're building camps *now*. Not that they had built a bunch of said camps *before* pulling the plug on most of humanity, nor had they been ready to hunker down while the monsters did their dirty work for them. No, they'd been forced to react to it all, too, so something hadn't gone according to plan, or not all the way to plan. Something stinks there, and I'm again glad we declined to go with them. Plus, there's Morgan to consider. She reacts about as well to following rules and orders all the time as a rock tossed into the lake and being told to swim. And I know who would have been caught in the middle of all that: me, as usual.

Still drowsy and warm but content to stay awake, I watch Eve sleep. It's not often you get to observe someone sleeping and (usually) at utter peace. I guess parents can do that with small children, but as adults, it's rare. The very fine lines that had started to emerge in the corners of her eyes during the day are gone, her hair is askew and covering one ear.

When we met, her dark-brown and straight hair had been around shoulder length, but now it spills down to the middle of her back. All the women have let their hair grow long over time and have lately been (rather exhaustively) discussing which of them is going to take over with styling and cutting when eventually needed. If they don't make up their minds soon, I'm going to put Bob in charge of all hair and see if that speeds things along.

Me, I'm good with long hair. I've always preferred it to short. I've even let mine go since I can't cut it (not well, anyway), and there isn't much point in doing so. It keeps the direct sun off my neck, and if I wet it down before going on a run or patrol, it cools me as it dries. That being said, I make sure to keep it away from my face in a practical clasp near the back of my head most of the time. Some of the younger guys had been doing man-bun nonsense before the zombies came, but their efforts to look like a ninja turned out, to my eyes, to make them resemble a soccer mom. Zombies, ninjas, and soccer moms ... hard to tell which of those are the most dangerous. I've been to restaurants and other businesses where one of the staff was assaulted by one of those—the soccer moms, I mean—and it had been pretty terrifying. There's probably a horror movie in there somewhere.

Only Bob keeps his hair short. He'd had a shaved head and goatee when we picked him up, along with Maya and Kuniko, and has stubbornly stuck with that, even if it mostly means shaving his head in the very cold water of the lake or waiting for the solar panels to warm some water for the job. He has loosened up a good bit since joining us and jokes about how the rest of us look like "fucking hippies" now, but it's always in a light-hearted way. He's happy with us and keeps busy every day, working on improvements to the cabins. After all, they're over a hundred years old now and have gone through that many New York winters, so there are boards to replace, endless screens to fix, water pumps to improve, and so on. I'm happy for his expertise as well as his willingness to teach because while I'm pretty handy, a lot of this stuff is out of my league.

Maya especially wears the guise of hippie well since her now-longer curly hair explodes from her head like someone who's gotten an electric shock, and any effort to tame it is a waste of time since there's always escapees. She also likes to wear baggy clothes when not patrolling or swimming, just loose, soft, and comfortable everything. All of that combined with her deep California tan makes her fit the part of a hippie rather well. I like Maya a lot—she's like another sister, but one who's a little less intense than my real one. There's an easy, simple groove to Maya that draws you to simply want to hang with her; there's no pretense or anything, she's just cool.

That very moment, she shuffles by outside the screen door, trailed by Amy, both of them holding steaming mugs of coffee and wearing the layers of clothing necessary in the mornings here, even in the summer. If you step outdoors without long sleeves and pants some days, it can be unpleasant, and goose bumps will blow up everywhere that isn't covered. Since Bob has rigged up a small bank of solar panels, we now have actual brewed coffee every morning, which is close to the best thing that could have happened aside from Eve coming to share the bed last night. Sadly, there's no real cream or milk to be had anymore, but if you want powdered flavored stuff, you have all you could ever, *ever* need available in the nearby stores.

Real coffee being a motivator, I slide out carefully from underneath Eve's arm and leave the room, closing the doors to the porch and the main room of the tiny cabin as I go. When I first met her, Eve would intermittently come to my bed but only for company and I guess modest comfort. She would sleep tucked tight against me but facing away. Last night, for the first time, she slept facing me and even threw an arm across my chest. She was so deeply out that she also drooled rather a bit on my shoulder, but I won't tell anyone.

Ajax snuffles over to say "hello" and then goes to wait by the glass front door for me to let him out. I collect a mug in the shape of a pig's head—my grandfather had been a big pig fan, though we never figured out why—and walk quietly out to sit with the girls, saying a sleepy "good morning." It's a nice, clear, and cool start to the day, like most of them are up here in the latter part of summer. The weather is going to accelerate into fall soon, and I'm mindful of how unpleasant it was last year with a smaller group. It's going to be less fun with the bunch of us in tighter quarters. Winter does not fool around in upstate New York … no, sir.

As if reading my mind, Amy speaks up from somewhere inside the gray oversized Vanderbilt hoodie she likes to wear all the time. "It's getting colder. Can we, like, move to the beach? I've never seen the ocean, aside from pictures on the internet and television. I had a dream last night that we were all somewhere on the beach, and it was warm and windy, and we were all happy. I'd like to build a sandcastle and get a tan and stuff. It was nice. And there were none of *them*."

Maya nods enthusiastically. "Yeah, I really miss the beach too. I'm always happy and content there. California girl and all, you know. I want to surf again and run in the sand, play volleyball, look for seashells, and smell the ocean. Even if it was here on the East Coast, though, I'd want to go south, maybe to the Carolinas? I don't want to go back to California. There were way too many of those fucking zombies out there. Are the beaches on this side any good? Sorry, Amy."

Amy had snickered when Maya swore, and pipes up before I can answer. "It's okay, I know all the words. My foster parents swore all the time, and I did ride the school bus, too, you know. When do I get to curse?" she asks, looking at me.

I'm not her dad, but in some regard, she treats me as such.

That's a great question too. "You know what? Any time you want," I answer.

What difference is it going to make? She has to be prepared to kill a zombie, or one of the kinds of people we've run into who are on the wrong side, has already learned how to drive—and back in the old days, those things kind of went hand in hand; cursing and driving, not zombies and driving—so who gives a shit if she swears?

"That's *fucking* awesome," the kid says with a monstrous, mischievous grin on her face. "I've been waiting to say 'shit' out loud a bunch of times since it's a fun word."

It sounds a little wrong coming out of her mouth because I've never heard her curse before and thanks to the youth in her voice, but it's also funny in a good-enough way, and we all giggle together.

The door opens, and Eve steps out, hair still mussed, coffee mug gripped firmly in her hand. Looking fabulous, by the way, in that subtle way she draws your eyes. "What's so funny, you three?"

We tell her and then say Maya is asking about the Carolina beaches. She smiles and sighs longingly. "Oh, the beach. I love the beach too. What about Hilton Head? I used to go there for golf tournaments a lot, back ... well, back then. It's beautiful there."

Hilton Head. I went there once with some buddies for a bachelor weekend, and while the golfing had been great, there weren't a lot of places for a bunch of young guys to get into any real trouble afterward. Topless bars didn't seem to exist, sadly, but that means if we go there now, we won't run into any half-dressed zombies, so there's that. Of all the weird things nowadays, that would be, well, *really* weird.

I recall Hilton Head is a huge island by comparison to some of the other coastal ones scattered on the edges of the Carolinas. Island is good since that means the monsters won't have many ways to get there other than causeways, and if I remember right, there's only one. Well two, one each for east- and westbound traffic, but that's it. We could figure something out to barricade it maybe. We have Bob the Engineer after all. There are lots of golf courses, tennis courts, running and biking paths, miniature golf courses, too, and plenty of green areas and nice beaches. Plus, given the population size and tourist invasions, there are a lot of grocery stores, so we'll be well supplied for food. There may be some monsters still around, of course, but we're good at removing those, and if we're systematic and cautious about it, we can probably clear the island thoroughly without too much effort.

My grandparents used to do the snowbird thing from here to the Florida beaches, usually coming and going around the Memorial and Labor Day weekends. Why not do the same? We'll be a little tight in the big Ford pickup and Morgan's Corvette, but it isn't like cars are hard or expensive to acquire anymore. The only problem we'll likely run into is a dead battery or flat gas, but we can just choose the next one down on the dealer's lot until we hit pay dirt. I find myself warming to the idea, especially faced with the forthcoming winter.

*Warming to the idea. Of the beach. You are clever! You should start doing stand-up.*

Sigh. Good thing the voice in my head stays mostly inside my head.

Everyone else drifts outside their cabins over the next little while, and we discuss it as a group, just like we did when the army had offered their version of sanctuary. We're a pretty democratic group in general, though at the end, it always seems like the heads all turn to me for the final decision. I hear the bubbling energy in their voices and watch the excitement liven each of their tired faces as they chat about what we can do down there, and know this is an easy call. Unlike back in the old days at work, when decisions needed to be analyzed, socialized, pragmatized, and agonized, we're just going to do what we want.

We're going to the beach.

# CHAPTER 3

**B**ut not all of us are going right away. Once the decision is made, Morgan is immediately impatient to hit the road, and I know how it will go if I try to keep her here, so after some quick discussion and map reading, we plan out her quick departure. The library a few towns over is open 24/7 now, and we have found a good selection of road atlases to reference, mostly for local roads but we now dig into the East Coast more thoroughly. Morgan and Bob will take Jack, go first, and scout the route and the island itself.

The rest of us, Kuniko, Maya, Eve, Amy, and me, will stay and pack as quickly and thoroughly as possible. Ajax will stay with us. We'll bring food, water from the spring in every container we have, all our guns, ammunition, other weapons, camping-type gear, and spare gas cans full to the brim since the truck is thirsty. Basically, everything we can think of and will fit in the vehicles is going to come south with us.

Having a dog with each group is critical since their wonderful noses pick up zombies way before we hear or see them, though it'll mean Jack is going to be squeezed a bit in the back of the Corvette, and they'll be limited for supplies.

"That's not a problem," Morgan says. "We're going to be moving fast anyway, *really* fast, so we can travel light outside of the basics. That okay with you, old man?" she asks Bob with a little smirk. While she has mellowed a little, the competitive chip on her shoulder about everything is firmly in place.

"Don't you worry about me, princess. I'll be fine."

She blanches at being called "princess" since she's about as non-girlie as can be, but for once, she keeps the sharp retort I know is brewing under wraps. I decide I'm glad I'm going with the other group since it seems like the two of them have some things to work out on the road trip.

We'll meet just off-island in Bluffton, South Carolina, whether the island is safe or not. If not, we'll go as a group farther south to check out other islands until we hit somewhere good. Also agreed is the route both groups will take, which is mostly going to be a series of interstates: 81 to 77 to 26 to 95. We took this more inland route on the way from North Carolina, and that had been fairly clear and less populated and, therefore, less monstered.

From a scouting perspective, if Bob and Morgan run into trouble in Pennsylvania, for example, they'll backtrack a few miles to safety to wait for us so we won't run into the very same trouble. No driving at night for anyone either.

My group will lock all the cabins up, store the key back in the outhouse under the seating platform where we know we'll find it—and where it's highly unlikely anyone else will; after all, who's going to reach their hand down into the crapper? And that'll be it for the upstate New York chapter.

The old BMW is going to stay here too. While it would be another vehicle and reduce the crowding, it's pretty old, and Ned only just got it running before using it to lead the monsters here for their slaughter, so I'm not confident we can rely on it for such a long trip. Maybe we'll come back someday.

Part of me resists all this, the part that loves it here—it may be the little kid in me, hiding under the accumulated years of life, especially the last few—but if it's safe at Hilton Head, it could be really great. The world is pretty much our oyster these days, so if we can re-create the relative security we've found here in a different, larger—and warmer, don't forget warmer—place, it's worth the shot. I love the beach, but vacation was an infrequent thing for me in the past when working; I'd take days here and there but no big chunks, usually just long weekends to squeeze a quiet round of golf in or take a drive or just sleep in. As a result, I haven't been to the coast as often as I could or should have when living in the Charlotte area, and I now find I'm eagerly looking forward to it too. Despite our now-happy crowd, the ghosts of DeeDee, Top, Amelie, and even Mabel have troubled me from time to time here, and I know it's time to tell them "goodbye" and move forward.

\*\*\*

Given Morgan's impatience and urge to be in motion, the red Corvette is quickly packed and idling in the driveway, sounding anxious to be underway itself. Not the most practical after-the-zombies kind of car, but it's gorgeous and wicked all at the same time. While she makes a face at me when I pull her to the side, Morgan promises not to dump Bob on the side of the road on their trip, no matter how annoyed she gets. Bob is pretty chill and I think they'll do fine, but it never hurts to ask her nicely. I'm pretty sure she gives me the finger when I turn around, but she'll stand by her promises.

Because I'm disappointed to leave the BMW and the inherent charisma of an older car behind, I decide when we get to the beach and settle, I'm going to start a car collection like the world has never seen, and I'm going to actually drive all of them unlike the collectors who were hoarding and auctioning them off in the past. Cars are meant to be driven, and in these times, I'm going to drive the tires off a bunch of whatever go-fast beasts I can get my hands and feet on. Hilton Head should be loaded with modern, high-dollar cars, and I hope I'll also be able to uncover some 1960s and '70s muscle cars in local houses as well.

Quick hugs all around and repeating the plans, and they're gone in a grumble of the fabulous V8, though carefully on the long, bumpy dirt and gravel driveway. While the others drift back toward their cabins to begin packing duties, I wait alone in the parking area near the burn barrel and outhouse, breathing in the childhood smells of here—not so much the outhouse—and guessing how long it'll take Morgan to reach the main road, and what she'll do when she gets there.

A couple of minutes later I find out. With the new silence dominating the world, I'm able to hear that she does what I expect: she absolutely hammers the gas pedal the second she reaches asphalt. The fantastic howl of the Corvette creeps up the hill to bathe me in the thunder of its exhaust and engine, even from over a mile away. *Chirp* go the tires as she hits second and third gear, and then the sound fades as they head farther away. Knowing Morgan, she's thinking if she can run about 100 miles an hour the whole way, they'll be there late this afternoon. Ten-ish hours at 100 miles an hour cooped up in the car with my sister. That *is* an adventure. I hope they get along well enough. I've been on road trips with Morgan in the past, and it isn't always easy to be contained for a long time with her.

# CHAPTER 4

Morgan is happy again. Mostly. The drive from Colorado had been good for her, though aside from meeting Jack-the-pirate and the short detour to Marcus's compound of horror, it was a boring drive on open highways through flatlands the whole time. But the freedom of the road, and the lack of a speed limit or any other rules, was invigorating. Having a destination, of any kind, keeps her ever-churning mind occupied, and as such, the moment they'd agreed to try the beach, she was practically in the car and halfway there. While the relative safety of the lake and environs is mostly a good thing, the thrill of the recent battles and utter freedom they give her to fight, dominate, and kill her opponents provides the liberation she's been seeking her entire life, and she knows staying there will make her stir-crazy if it remains quiet and safe. Moving somewhere, anywhere, increases the chances of finding the next challenge.

It's going to take a couple of hours to get to one of the major highways, and everything in between is a two-lane, curvy dream of a road for a car like the Corvette. Like always, she can and will test her limits at their very edges, and if Bob is uncomfortable along the way, well, that's just too bad since he volunteered to come along. She preferred to go alone, but her brother had insisted. This put her in a bit of a mood, but the thought of flying down the road for many hours in the magnificent Corvette assuaged her vague resentment of his company. Bob is something of a mystery to her; he's all the things she's not. He's, like, old, somewhere around fifty, and not physically capable like her. And bald. And he's a quiet, analytical sort who watches and studies everything before taking action or speaking. She's fine with quiet but not with being studied, as it makes her uneasy, and it's going to be a long drive no matter how things go between the two of them. She hopes for the best and promises herself to at least try and hold her tongue. A little.

After peeling away from the foot of the hill leading away from the lake, Morgan runs up through the gears a little roughly, letting the subtle brutality of the car's acceleration ease some of the pent-up energy she needs to burn off. She's been content enough here; having her brother nearby has always been the one constant source of solace in her life, and her relief at finding him alive and then fighting with him side by side has filled a space in her she didn't know existed. This new world allows unfettered Morgan to be free; it's something she has been looking for without knowing it's out there to be found.

Guiding the car through the first handful of miles at well over the bold 55 posted on the roadside signs, shifting up and down as she sees fit and accelerating at every straightaway to maximum speed before braking heavily for the corners, she notices Bob looking down toward her legs rather than out the windshield at the blur of upstate New York whizzing by the open windows. While she's accustomed to being looked at by men, and has been since she was a middle teen, she bristles at it now. Bob is supposed to be one of the good guys, and if he's going to be staring at her for the next few days like a typical drooling male ape, this isn't going to work for her at all. She tries to ignore it for another mile or two, but he keeps looking over, and, finally, she can't take it. So much for promises.

"Stop it," she says as nicely as she can. It isn't *that* nicely, but she deserves a small nod for effort.

"Stop what?"

"You know what. You're staring at me. Don't be an asshole. Keep it up, and you're walking to the beach or back up the hill."

Bob doesn't answer immediately, but when he does, she's surprised. "Wow. That escalated quickly from road trip buddies to bitch in the driver's seat. I'm not staring at you, not like you think anyway. It's not always about you, Morgan, even though you think it always is. Get over yourself."

Anger flares deep inside her, and if they weren't going eighty, she would have hit him right then. Jack must have sensed the change in atmosphere since he perks up his head from the back space and looks between the two humans. She slams on the brakes and brings the car sharply to a stop across both lanes of the road, hits the button to turn off the engine, and hops out of the car. "Screw you, Bob! I've seen you staring at my legs and who knows what else. You need to cut it out."

He climbs out of the car, too, and lifts his sunglasses to perch atop his bald head as she's talking, and now he laughs at her. Hard. Which really doesn't help matters and also confuses the crap out of her. "Oh, you really *do* need to get over yourself. I wasn't staring at your legs like that. I was watching how you drove and wondering how you got your license in the first place and haven't killed yourself since. You're a lousy driver for a car like this. Driving it like you're mad at it. Keep *that* up, and we won't make it to the beaches."

He stares at her over the bright-red roof. Morgan is boiling mad indeed, and it's a good thing the car is between them. Jack breaks the moment for a second by hopping out and wandering over to water a plant on the side of the road.

"Give me the keys," Bob says. "I'll show you how a car like this should be driven."

"Kiss my ass. I'd rather eat gas station sushi," she snaps.

"Again, get over yourself. I bet most people *have* kissed your ass over the years, literally and figuratively. I don't want anything from you other than a successful trip to South Carolina and maybe some companionable conversation along the way. Calm down, give me the dang keys, and be a grown-up."

Morgan is so angry, she can't think of what to say, and it's a good thing since she slows down (just a little) and thinks. He had been looking at her when she shifted, and had definitely been only looking in the footwell, not her midsection or above. Maybe she's wrong. She throws the

keys at him, harder than she needs to across six feet of car and right at his face. "I don't need to give you the keys, jackass. It's a push-button start."

Bob snags the key fob effortlessly out of the air and smiles. "It's symbolic, you cranky brat. Settle down and get in the car. I'm trying to teach you something, to help you. Jesus, hasn't it been exhausting, being ready to be pissed off your whole life? Always looking for the worst in people? I bet you find it all the time when you look at the world that way. I know it's tiring and depressing to be around someone like that," he says with a pointed look at her and then whistles for Jack, who has been wandering across an open, grassy space. Jack trots over, noses Morgan's hand, and hops back in the car, tongue wagging and ready to go.

"Just drive," Morgan grumbles as they switch sides and seats.

He drops his glasses back to the bridge of his nose and nudges the ignition button. After studying and flipping a series of switches on the dashboard, he smiles wickedly at her, tells her to hang on, and then, boy, does he drive.

Morgan isn't accustomed to feeling fear; even in the current reality where most outcomes are living or dying and that's it, it has been rare. She fights over the course of the next ten miles to avoid giving Bob the satisfaction of knowing he's scaring the ever-loving crap out of her, grasping the sides of the seats as subtly but firmly as possible, in a death grip of holy-shit-we're-going-to-die-in-this-next-corner. The odd thing is he makes it look effortless, charging with abandon into turns and feathering the throttle to keep the car completely under control, barely braking and then mashing the gas at just the right point to burst out of the apex in a thunderous roar, allowing the sports car to do exactly what it has been built for. No real squeal of tires at any point to indicate he got the timing or angle wrong, just a desperate mad dash across the countryside and harmonic symbiosis of driver and car.

He finally coasts to a stop, straddling the double yellow line, and touches the button to turn the car off again. They sit there for a minute, listening to the tick of the hot metal of the exhaust and sudden silence after the howling banshee of the car's assault on the rural farmland roads. Morgan's finally able to relax her hands and finds them slightly cramped from the effort, but she manages and then steps out of the car again.

Bob does, too, and tosses her the keys over the roof, much more gently than she had. His tone is softer as well now. "That's how you drive a car. It's a partnership, not a battle to beat it into submission. You work with the car, feel it out, get a sense of what it can do, and then once you get all of it right, it's like watching two experts dance. It's an amazing thing to behold, as you just saw if you were able to keep your eyes open the whole time," he says with a kind smirk, pauses for a second, and then continues. "You know, that's kind of how people stuff works too. You ought to give it a chance someday. We're all friends here. You saved our lives. None of us are out to get you, or hurt you, or screw you over."

He walks around the car's nose and grins one more time. "And yeah, your legs are fine. Don't let it go to your head though."

"Jerk," she replies, not unkindly.

Ice firmly broken, they hit the road, heading southeast and going fast.

# CHAPTER 5

Thunder is common in North Carolina in the summer. Hell, the weather forecasters would be pretty safe coming on the air in early May as follows: "Folks, it's going to be hot, humid, and with a good chance of thunderstorms from now until October. See you in a few months." It could happen any day, seemingly spontaneously, and I've heard it at any time of the day too. Morning t-storms are rare but possible. Thunderstorms in upstate New York are practically unheard of, at least in the years Morgan and I came up as kids and over the time we've been here in the present. But my many years in North Carolina are why I'm slow to pay full attention on the day after Morgan and Bob leave, just after sunrise sneaks over the eastern edge of the tree line, casting faint color to the day. I'm in the driveway, shuffling around some of the stuff in the bed of the pickup to fit better, and hear the rumble once, twice but distant and somehow not from above. Ajax is keeping me company and tilts his head to the left, listening, and then jogs lightly off to do the morning necessaries.

As it continues for longer than you subconsciously expect from thunder, I finally stop what I'm doing and listen more closely. It isn't thunder, it's warfare. Artillery maybe, some explosions anyway, and then small arms thrown in for good measure. A *lot* of small arms fire. Morgan and I grew up within earshot of Camp Smith in the very outer suburbs that reached New York City via car-plus-train commute, and from time to time, they would carry on artillery exercises— the camp, not the city—and if the wind was right, we could sometimes hear them blowing stuff up. That had been an organized sound, if artillery barrages could be called "organized," since they probably planned out everything for targeting, sequence, and duration. This is chaotic, sporadic, and as I listen, almost desperate sounding. I don't like it; it sounds like whoever has all those guns is losing, which is unsettling. It keeps going, hammering at the sky and echoing across the lake, and the rest of my crowd wanders outside, looking up and around for the right direction.

"What is that?" asks Amy. "It sounds like a fight, and a big one. It must be the army guys who came here, maybe?"

"I guess so since who else could it be?" I answer. "But I figured they were gone since we didn't join them. That's not a good sound though. Fighting means zombies, and that much noise for that long means a lot of them. And the explosions running down means the zombies are winning or all dead. But either way, it's time. We finish packing what we can in the next hour and leave. Sorry about the crappy wake-up and short breakfast, but we have to go. I'm going to head to the top of the hill and see if I can tell which direction it's coming from, and we're going to go the other way."

Everyone scatters back to the cabins, anxious to grab anything else we haven't already put together for the trip and with an urgency in their step that's good to see. The truck needs to stay here so they can pack, so I'll run the driveway.

I'm about to call Ajax to me and go when Eve stops me. "Shouldn't we go see what happened? If they won, that would be good, but even if they lost, and there are survivors? Or maybe some things we can use if the zombies won but left. Like bigger guns and other stuff? The army has all kinds of mines and bombs and food supplies, right?"

She has a good point. I'm not convinced there are going to be survivors—one side or the other is probably wiped out completely, and based on the sounds, my bet's on the monsters. It's not like the zombies to stop, and I bet the military guys won't either, but gathering some heavier weapons has some allure, especially explosives. My improvised bomb had worked well for mass monster destruction back in North Carolina, so I nod and say I'm going to scout quickly to see if I can tell what direction the noise is coming from and to check for anything potentially headed our way. We'll go see what happened as soon as I get back, all together in the truck, then leave immediately after that, no matter what. I pull a shotgun from the front porch, check for ammo, and then call Ajax, and we haul ass up the driveway, spraying gravel from my shoes since I feel a combination of urgency and foreboding. If there's a wave of zombies big enough to wipe out the army guys, and they're headed our way, we're in beyond deep shit.

The sprint up the driveway to the main road goes by in a blur, and I coast to a jog and then full stop just under the edge of the trees shading the entrance and look off into the distance, scanning. Hard to miss it—to the east is a ragged, billowing pillar of dense smoke licking the base of the rising sun, obscuring what would have been a clear sunrise. I watch, not that I'm going to see anything specific since it looks a few miles away, but because I don't know what else to do. There's a final, weak *thump* from that direction, and then I hear it. Faint from this far away but unmistakable.

*Muuuuuuuhhhhh!*

Sounds like the army lost. I turn back around and fly toward the cabins. We need to go, now.

***

By the time I get back, everyone's as ready as can be, so we pile into the truck after locking up the cabins and taking a wistful last look at the still waters lapping at the edges of our sanctuary. Maybe we'll be back, but the reality of a force of monsters large enough to (probably) wipe out the army people makes it unlikely. Eve sits in the front seat next to me, and Amy, Kuniko, and Maya squeeze into the back. Ajax basically sits in Eve's lap, head out the window and tongue lolling as we drive out toward the main road. The dog weighs about as much as Eve does, so it can't be all that comfortable for her, but she doesn't seem to mind. All of our crap is in the back; it's road-trip time again, and we're good at assembling our gear, starting with weapons first, then water, then spare gas in some jerry cans we've been using for a while, and then more weapons. Food will be no trouble to get along the way, though we have some with us, and Amy is quickly devouring the last of the blueberries in the back, juice dribbling down her chin.

The smoke of the battle is still rising as we drive, and I tell everyone to be on alert and looking in every direction. I think about Top describing his base's invasion by the zombies, where they'd simply been unprepared and overrun. These guys have known about the possibility and seems like they've lost, too, which isn't a good sign. An alpha? More than one? Or just so many bad guys—I guess I'm referring to the zombies, not army, but that's a blurry line now given what the colonel told us about who's responsible for the bright and shiny new world we're fighting to survive in—that they overwhelmed the military could be possible too. None of it is encouraging, and I feel my heart racing along with anxiety, and I'm glad when Eve reaches across the cab and slides a hand into mine and squeezes once. I remind myself that no matter what, we have a four-wheel-drive truck and can elude and outrun a force of zombies if needed. Unless they've learned how to drive—that would be a thing. But assuming no for now, in this one instance, we aren't going to be forced to fight as long as we see them first and are going to run if there's any danger.

As we reach the main road that sits at the base of the fairly shallow valley, we pause at the stop sign. Not because I'm worried about traffic, but the smoke is off to the right, which is the opposite direction of where we need to go if we're going to follow Morgan and Bob and simply head toward the beach. Part of me wants to skip checking out what has happened, but the idea of possible survivors and heavier weapons makes me reluctantly turn the wheel to the right.

*You know that this is what happens in horror movies, right? Of* course *the basement without windows or doors is the best place to hide. Yes, you should* definitely *lock the doors to your car when getting out, so that when you're chased by the monster du jour, you have to fumble with the keys to make things exciting. One of these days, you'll learn to be a little more selfish, like I keep telling you to try on for size.*

We pass through the town that has been a near-constant source of sorrow—the collection of bodies in the grocery-store freezer, and the mass of critters Ned brought to try and kill us—and continue east for another couple of miles, following the chimney of smoke that's now weakening but still giving us a touchstone to pursue. There's a breeze behind us that's pushing the smoke away slowly, and we finally come around a gentle bend in the road, up a rise, and then we see it. The camp is below the road and in the very center of one of the valley's sprawling and neglected farms. It was quickly yet carefully built, but now it is a scene of utter devastation. I stop the truck, leaving it running (thank you, inside voice), and we all wordlessly climb out.

A perimeter fence surrounds a roughly five- to six-acre space and is secured to vertical metal posts every fifteen feet or so, topped by several courses of razor wire tilted to the exterior. A second, shorter fence is recessed another twenty feet inside the first. Both fences are shrouded in bodies, both zombies and military, dangling like Christmas ornaments from the razor wire and floating heavily in the breeze. One huge fifty-foot-wide section of the fence is flattened, as if it was run over by a steamroller, and fans of bodies litter both the exterior and interior of it. Hundreds and hundreds of corpses are scattered in every direction. It's easy to see where the army men were forced to make a stand since I can see piles of zombie bodies leading to a single soldier's remnants in a dozen locations throughout the camp.

It's terrifying to think about how they must have felt since I know, but not on this scale since it had to have been a thousand or more that attacked. A thousand people is a lot in a smallish space. A thousand zombies intent on ripping you to human confetti and devouring whatever's left is something else entirely. The zombies never stop. Ever. Shoot an arm off? No problem, they have another to grab you with. Blast a leg to smithereens? They'll hop and drag or crawl, still trying to get you. Shoot their head? Then you're good. But otherwise, I bet these poor kids had ultimately panicked when all their training, weapons superiority, and walls failed them, and they were overrun by an enemy that's worse than anything the world has ever seen.

Vehicles smolder everywhere, too, parked helter-skelter throughout the "roads" inside the camp. The breeze keeps pulling the smoke off to the east, and I'm glad since I have a feeling it smells pretty bad here, too; if not now, then for sure in a day or two. Craters encircle the fences, smallish ones about ten feet across and a few feet deep, which must have been all the heavier explosions I heard. Red smears stain the dusty, trampled ground like the beginning of an obscene abstract painting.

Nothing is moving other than the smoke and the flickering of the small fires dotting across our view. We wait for a solid five minutes, scanning for motion both within the camp and out to the edges of our vision in case the wave that crashed over and through the soldiers comes back. I watch Ajax, too, who's alert but not I-smell-monsters alert, so I take that as a good sign. "We need to go see if anyone is alive. I don't want to go down there, I really don't, but we should check."

"I don't know," Eve says. "Nothing is moving, but what if some of the zombies are hurt enough to be kind of dormant, and our scent wakes them up?"

I really want to just leave, but I feel the draw of Eve's earlier suggestion to see if there's anyone alive. Plus, bigger and better weapons *have* to be down there, and I want some of that if we can find anything that will add to our firepower.

"I agree with Eve," Maya pipes up. "Let's go down and see what we can see. Nothing's going on. It's safe." With that, she hops easily over the shallow drainage ditch beside the road and jogs toward the destroyed camp.

We all follow after gathering as many weapons from the bed of the truck as we can carry. Something bothers me as I watch Maya's graceful passage across the unmarked fields and closer to the fence line, but it doesn't immediately come to me … and then it does.

*The craters. You weren't hearing artillery before. There aren't any artillery pieces down there. What sense would those make anyway? Those are for killing from a long distance, and zombie killing is strictly a close and personal business. Those craters are from mines around the perimeter.*

*No!*

I scream Maya's name and take off in a mad sprint since she's well ahead of us by now, and I'm not sure she hears me since she doesn't even pause. Ajax is on my heels and doesn't race ahead but just keeps pace. She's about fifty yards ahead of me, and I can only watch as she jumps lightly over a tiny stream that trickles through the center of the valley, lands with the athleticism we've seen, takes two more steps, and …

*WHA-BOOM!*

She vanishes.

The concussion is a sharp, sudden blast of sound that thunders the air and feels like I've been clapped on the side of the head by a giant. Dirt and grass fountain into the sky and across the trampled grass, along with what little is left of Maya. A bloody mist rises to join the drifting smoke, and I stumble to a jagged stop. I'm ahead of everyone else and close enough so that a rain of blood, bits of bone, and other pieces of her splash in a crescent pattern to sprinkle me in a sheen of crimson. I'm weak in the knees and heart. *Not another one*, I think, *not so soon after we've brought them out of the trap in Kansas.* My heart feels wrenched from my chest, and I fall to my knees, resting my hands on the red-stained soil but conscious now that the mines could be anywhere. I at least have the presence of mind to yell for everyone to freeze when I hear them coming up behind me. Eve staggers to a stop next to me, sobbing. Kuniko and Amy are right behind her, and we all just sit there, watching the debris of the explosion settle back to the ground, trying not to look at the unrecognizable pieces of our friend smashed to bits and scattered across the farmland in a sickening rain of horror.

"*No!*" screams Kuniko abruptly, louder than anything I've ever heard from her, even through the fog of my newly muffled hearing. It's like listening to everything through a thick towel, but her shrieks come through in piercing cries that tear at my heart.

She lunges to go past me, to help someone who is beyond help—someone who isn't even a someone anymore—and I grab her arm and pull her back. She pelts me with her hands and fists, trying to get free, and I pinion her arms finally, drawing her into an awkward hug to hold and settle her down. "No, the mines, there have to be more. You can't help her. She's gone."

Amy just stands there, mouth agape and tears sheeting down her checks. She saw Ned die, and maybe one or two more back at the beginning of the end, but Maya was one of "us," one of our people. Amy, too, then totters and drops to her knees after a moment.

I'm devastated. The cool California kid just simply evaporated right in front of me, and if I'd been the one in the lead, like most days, I would now be spread all over the ground instead. My hands are shaking as I regain my feet, and I begin to move backward, dragging the weeping

Kuniko, back on the route I traveled to try and catch Maya since I know it's safe from other mines.

We collect ourselves and just stand there after retreating a hundred yards or so. My ears are ringing, and the world sounds flat and hollow, not that anyone is doing a lot of talking. I can't believe it. They surrounded the camp with mines, which is smart of course, but somehow, the hundreds or however many monsters who wiped the soldiers off the face of the earth had missed that one. Or more. Shit. Shit. Shit!

"We need to leave. I want to go away. Now please," says Amy through the cotton balls blocking my ears.

I agree with her and am ready to move farther back toward the truck and find a towel or something to clean me off when Eve partially raises a hand and waves it toward the ground to shush us. "Wait. Everyone, be quiet. Do you hear that?"

I obviously can't but try anyway. Kuniko stops snuffling against my chest and tilts her head toward the disaster area inside the fence, as does Amy. Ajax has perked his head up, too, though how his hearing's okay is beyond me since he'd been right beside me when the mine went off, and his ears have to be in agony from the explosion.

"It's a tapping, banging sound. From over there by those vehicles," Eve says, pointing to a handful of drab green trucks and Humvees, along with a single armored personnel carrier flipped on its side and bearing a few new-looking dents and scrapes near the back door.

*Um, maybe here is where you take a minute to think about what the hell was strong enough to turn one of those over, sunshine? See? I was right. You morons just ran to the basement when the horror movie bad guy was chasing you. It is so time to leave. The kid is smarter than the rest of you put together.*

Good point, though the flattened fences prove that whatever had come through here wasn't some small group looking for a snack. No, it had to be a huge force that would make a big racket, but the voice inside is making a pretty convincing argument. Whatever's making a noise is "over there," and between here and there could be dozens more mines. No thanks.

"It's someone who needs help," Amy notes.

"You're right, Amy," Eve replies. "Someone survived all of this, and they heard the explosion and know someone is here."

Kuniko remains silent, eyes glassy and vacant, which makes sense since she knew Maya longer than the rest of us and had the shared, shitty experience of Marcus's horror house to bond them. I ease her to a sitting position on the grass and rest a hand on her shoulder, trying to keep providing some comfort.

Eve turns to me, and I know what's coming. "We have to try and help whoever that is. I think they're trapped inside that thing on its side."

"That's a nice thought, but in case you missed it, one of our friends got blown to smithereens about a minute ago, and where there is one mine, there are lots of mines," I answer, not intending the sarcastic and biting tone I use, but

I'm deeply upset. I feel like I've let us down somehow, that my job as protector has been done badly. Plus, I was really fond of Maya. I have lost people from my group before, but thinking on it now, it was never in front of me due to violence like this. DeeDee's death had been almost peaceful as she ran out of air, and Top, Amelie, and Mabel had died away from the cabins in their battles with the monsters. This … this is something new for me, and I don't like it. At all.

"Don't be a jerk. Of course I noticed. We're all upset, not just you. But we have to figure out how to get in there and see if we can help."

I look around my now-smaller tribe and see Amy and Kuniko are nodding too. Shit. Sure, let's go wandering through a minefield to save people who may or may not have directly participated in the intentional slaughter of pretty much the entire human race. There is taking forgiveness a step too far, but I know we're going to try.

There are roughly another hundred yards from where we stand to the outside ring of fencing. The mines aren't going to be inside the fence, and there has to be some kind of safe path from inside the camp to outside for the vehicles and people to get in and out. I don't see any flags or other markings, nor can I see any trampled-down areas that indicate there has been some repeated traffic across it. Pretty much everything is mashed to the turf thanks to the horde that swept through here, leaving a swathe of death in its wake. Tiptoeing through the tulips and hoping for the best won't work either, and I rack my brain as I look around for how to get us across the killing zone safely. Unload the truck of all our gear, set it in drive, and let it roll across to see if there are more mines in its path? Not a bad idea except if it hits a mine quickly, we won't know what's beyond that and will only be slightly closer but out of options. And the truck could miss a mine lurking between the tires, and that would make for a nasty surprise. I'm not worried about us since we would walk in the tire tracks, but Ajax may not and could take us all out with a badly placed paw. We could probably get other vehicles without too much trouble—and we have the BMW, though it would be cozy with four humans and Ajax, and we'd have to leave supplies behind—but I rule that out since we aren't close to any houses or the town.

Since the mines are clearly pressure sensitive, we have to figure out how to trip any remaining ones and then (damn carefully) go through that same area. Do they need a certain amount of weight? Will they play possum if the pressure is low, like five pounds, so that if a squirrel or rabbit wanders across it, it won't go off as a false alarm and wild overkill? I have no clue, and all the people who would know are sprawled across my line of sight, torn into bits and pieces.

This is frustrating. We can hear the tapping across the open space that may as well have been a mile away, and some muffled yelling. I'm stumped, and tired, and emotionally wrought, so I sit down on a nearby stone wall. Stone walls are ubiquitous up here—they're everywhere, marking the division of properties or crop sections. Ajax trots over, takes a leak on a couple of slate-colored rocks farther down the line, and then lies at my feet in the sunlight now creeping fully over the horizon to warm the day. The rocks are cool under my backside and hands, and I subconsciously lift one of the smaller ones from the top and turn it over in my hands as my brain is turning over the problem.

Kuniko has gone back to get the truck and drives it down closer to us, being careful to follow the same route we all had, and then brings a bottle of water over to me. Some of the stones from the wall had tumbled off over the years to lay in the grass, and as she gets close to me, her toe catches on one of those, and she stumbles. The water bottle flies out of her hand as she gets ready to catch herself, and my rock falls out of mine as I spring to my feet and reach for her. In tandem, I catch her, and the bottle falls to the ground, and the rock promptly falls on top of it. The bottle bursts, even though the cap is still on, and I realize we've just found the solution.

\*\*\*

We spend the next two hours playing a modified version of beanbags or cornhole, depending on where you're from, with higher stakes than normal. We've unloaded the extra gas cans since they're at the rear of the bed and are bulky, plus some of the camping-type gear so I will have room to stand. Moving the extra-explosive stuff when we're going to intentionally play with actual explosives seems like a good idea.

I back the truck up to face the compound and then stand on the tailgate while the women make a bucket brigade of sorts and bring me smaller rocks from the wall. The plan is to toss the stones out in a tight pattern, and that's why I need smaller ones about the size of a cantaloupe, so I can throw them far enough away from us. In case I do hit a mine, we won't be hit by any shrapnel or debris. It almost backfires on us right away since Ajax immediately wants to play fetch with the first one, just like he had during the most recent round of golf, but luckily, he stops as soon as I shout, "No!"

It's an exercise in throw, duck, and wince, and we prepare for either an ear-shattering *WHA-BOOM* or soft *thump*. I throw at least a dozen rocks out before hitting the first mine, which scares the shit out of us all over again. My arms are aching after a while, but no one else is strong enough to throw the stones far enough away, so I stick with it. Tasks are always good for me, even the mindless ones, and now the repetition and vague concentration keeps my mind off Maya. Every once in a while, the image of her being vaporized will flicker across my consciousness, but I try to fight that away as best as I can. The rest of the group is silent, too; everyone immersing themselves in the task rather than the recent reality.

We blow two more mines as we work, startled every time one of them goes off, creeping the truck slowly backward over the mock cobblestone road we're making as we clear, and finally reach the flattened fence line and, in theory, to safety. Everyone's hands are dry, chafed, and bleeding by that time, and so we rest a few moments and pour water over the skin to relieve some of the discomfort. My shoulders are howling bundles of pain, and I can barely lift them over my head. The girls are sweaty messes, too, hair plastered to their skulls, and perspiration soaking their shirts. The stone wall has been whittled down to what looks like broken teeth sporadically peeking out of the turf in both directions for a good hundred yards. I'm proud of us; no matter what happens, there's a gritty persistence to the group that keeps us all moving beyond when we would have all quit in the old days. Folks in the old days before our old days had been that way too. There wasn't such a thing as "too hard"; they had to get things done and, therefore, had to figure out how to perform the tricky tasks one way or another. That determination and innovation had been a lot of what had made the country great. The recent reliance on "there's an app for that" and what had felt like taking lazy shortcuts more than you should means that more people are dead now than might have been fifty years before. Maybe even twenty. Maybe I'm romanticizing the gumption of our ancestors, but I picture them facing off with the monsters better than modern men and women had. Their hands certainly would have been free from smartphones and fancy coffee cups and, therefore, readier to fight, but we're never going to find out. Here we are with a new kind of "too hard" problem to figure out on our own.

The tapping had stopped at some point; it's hard to say when because of the ringing in my ears from the collective concussions of the exploding mines. It feels like I've spent a weekend at an outdoor heavy metal festival, minus the Goth kids, tattoos, bad choices, and hangover, and I know I'll be sore tomorrow. Pretty much all over.

"Now what?" a clearly exhausted Amy asks from underneath the sweaty, ragged bush of hair hanging over her face.

"We take a few minutes to rest, get a drink, get some guns, and then see what's tapping. I'm guessing it's a soldier, but I can also see a zombie stuck inside the truck, hearing the explosion and smelling us somehow and bashing his fool head against a steel door to try and get at us. So, water, then guns. I don't think we should stick around for too long since the sound of those explosions would have carried well, and they could circle back if they're still within earshot."

After being ambushed recently by the alpha zombie, and bitten, after we'd been attacked at the cabins—thanks again, Ned, you asshole—plus seeing this devastation of people with guns, training, fences, and inside knowledge, I'm not planning on underestimating the monsters again.

I hear the tapping resume again, more urgently now, but we take our moment to rest and arm ourselves. I don't really think there's a zombie or two trapped in the armored personnel carrier, but I'm also not sure trusting the army is on the list of to-dos after what the colonel told us. Speaking of the colonel, I wonder if he's one of the ones inside, or if he's an indeterminate smear somewhere nearby. We cautiously walk to the APC and study the back door. It's bent near the clasps, dented in heavily. I can't think what might have done that, and I feel some anxiety. We're spending too much time here after making a lot of noise, and if the military has been wiped out here, what chance will we have?

"Hey! Is there someone out there? Help us, please!" comes a male voice from inside, then joined by a female one yelling indistinct words.

I answer, "Yeah, we're out here. Is there a crowbar or something around?"

"There should be some tools on the roof of this APC. Or maybe nearby?"

We scrounge around and eventually find a six-foot-long breaker bar in a dead soldier's hands, one end of it embedded in the center of a zombie's head at his feet. It's pretty grisly work prying it loose, and part of me keeps expecting the zombie to pop up and attack. I hand the shotgun to Kuniko and tell her to hold it right against its nose. I finally get it loose, trying not to look too closely at the goop drizzling off, and wedge it into one of the creases in the door opening of the APC.

"Please, hurry. We've been in here a long time, and it's hot, and we don't have much air," comes the plaintive female voice from inside.

"Okay, just hang on."

I push against the bar. Nothing except a faint groan of the hinges. I push harder and get a smidge of movement.

*Muuuuuuuhhhhh!*

Shit.

Not close, but not really far either.

Eve comes to help me with the bar, tucking herself inside my arms since she's small enough, and we both lean hard on it. Another creak, but nothing significant. A hand reaches out through the small space that's now open. A bloody, dirty, grasping hand, clutching at the edge of the door.

*Muuuuuuuhhhhh!*

Closer. And louder.

"Help us. Get us out of here!" Bodies may not get through the gap we've opened, but desperation sure can.

"What the fuck do you think we're trying to do?" I snap, conscious this is all going sideways in a hurry. "Amy and Kuniko, hop up on something and see what you can see. We need to know what kind of trouble we're about to be in. If this doesn't work, and they come into sight, we're gone."

Sorry, people inside the vehicle, but us first nowadays. I'm getting frustrated and more nervous, but we don't owe these people anything. They're the cause of all this if the colonel is to be believed, so I'm short on sympathy.

Amy scrambles on top of the APC and then hops across a small open space to stand atop the cab of an even larger camouflaged truck. "I see movement over that way," she says, pointing back to the west. "Coming out of the trees. I think we have a couple of minutes still, but you need to hurry."

What does everyone think I'm doing? Jesus. "Push from the inside. This door is so bent, we can't do it ourselves. You have about one minute before we're out of here, so push like your life depends on it because it does."

We lean back to the task, and Kuniko wiggles beside us, adding her weight too. We hear grunting inside as the troopers push, and the door jumps another couple of inches open. Not enough though.

*Muuuuuuuhhhhh!*

Amy starts to jump up and down nervously on top of the truck. "They're coming. Oh my God, there are so many of them!"

The growing panic in her voice is obvious, and while I want to look and see how far away they are, the fact that I can now hear the thunder of their footsteps tells me all I need to know, but I ask anyway through gritted teeth, "How many?"

"I think it's all of them."

Fuck. "One more push, and then we go. Hey, army people, get your shit together! This is it, so you better put everything you have into it."

We all lean, push, and swear, and the door finally pops open and slams against the side of the vehicle with a loud *clang.* Two soldiers covered in dirt, grease, and sweat blink into the light, carrying their weapons, and then Amy screams, "Run!"

We do without hesitation. The truck is twenty steps away, and we race toward and into it, everyone piling in, including the soldiers, who hop into the bed. I look in the side rearview mirror as I turn the ignition key, and immediately wish I hadn't.

*You know that thing about how objects in the rearview mirror are closer than they appear? Yeah, well, it's true. Move it, sunshine, or we're fucked! The gas pedal is the skinny one on the right. I suggest you find out how far toward the floor it'll go, like right now.*

A horde pours over a small rise in the farm's fields, filling my entire view, rushing at us at a dead run. Not as fast as people can sprint, but pretty damn close. Not good at all—that's new, but I don't have time to consider it right now. I fire the truck up, slam it into drive, and mash the gas pedal. It surges across the lumpy stone path we've made to get into the camp, bouncing everyone around like Ping-Pong balls in a lottery machine, but there's nothing for it. We bang and crash our way out toward the rest of our gear where I want to stop if we can, but just then, the soldiers in the back open up with their rifles.

"Go, go, go! They're right on us!"

*Muuuuuuuhhhhh!*

The automatic weapons answer in kind, shattering the day, and I hear spent shells pinging into the back of the truck as they fire. A glance in the mirror again shows me the monsters are starting to fall back behind as I accelerate, and I watch a handful of them go down in a bloody spray as the rapid-fire bullets hit home, shredding the front rank of our pursuers.

The truck fights for traction on the hillside that inclines up to the road, sliding sideways and churning the grass but not moving forward. I set it into four-wheel drive, and the big tires finally bite. We hop onto the road and accelerate for real, not looking back anymore, just going. New gear could be gathered along the way, but I regret losing some of it, and we weren't even able to pick up any of the military's weapons aside from whatever they have on them.

I'm shaking as I drive and concentrate on steadying my breathing. It has been a really shitty morning. And then it gets worse.

The dog.

Ajax isn't in the truck.

I slam on the brakes now that we're about a half mile away, hearing everyone bang around again and cursing. Doing the quick math that if they're still on our trail we have at least three or four minutes, I start to turn around.

"What are you *doing*?" Eve practically shouts at me, turning to look at me with real fear in her eyes.

I don't answer but swing the truck around onto the westbound lane and head back the way we came. We'd come up and over a shallow hill in the last few hundred yards, and I coast to a stop as we crest the peak of it. Below and in front of us is perhaps the most insane sight of all since the end of the world, which is saying something. Thousands of zombies spread across the flat bottom of the valley, a giant mass of former humanity running, stumbling, pinwheeling their arms, and reaching for my dog who frantically races ahead of them. He isn't far out of their reach but is opening the gap slowly. Normally, he'd fight and take a bunch of them down, but he's a smart dog and is hauling ass toward us as he sees the truck edge over the hill.

"We came back here for a dog? Are you out of your fucking mind? Turn this truck around now and get us out of here," says the male soldier.

And then of all things, I feel the still-warm barrel of his rifle against my neck. I ignore it at first, watching Ajax gallop across the field and begin the climb toward us, calculating the speed of his pursuers and thinking we're going to be okay.

"Sir," says the voice again, with greater pressure from the gun.

"Get that fucking gun off of me right now unless you want me to turn the truck off and break the key off in the ignition and leave us all up shit's creek. I pretty much owe that dog my life, and by my count, you owe me yours, so do something useful and shoot the ones close to him instead of being an asshole. And if you shoot the dog, I'm going to throw you out of the truck as a snack for them so the rest of us can get away!" I snap, meaning every word of it.

The pressure increases for a moment and then lifts off. I hear the soldier settle the rifle on top of the truck with a metallic *clunk*, and he begins firing, missing on the first shot but then the zombie closest to Ajax loses the top of his head, staggers another few steps, and collapses. The second rifle fires, too, picking one of the monsters off from the other side. They're good shots, making them count, and the leading pack of the mob chasing the dog dwindles quickly.

Ajax flies toward us, tongue hanging out of the side of his mouth and what looks like fear in his big eyes. Rottweilers aren't really runners, not for big distances or high speed, but he's moving like a greyhound right now. I throw my door open as he reaches us and grunt as one hundred twenty pounds of fur, muscle, and bone slams into and scrabbles across me to land on Eve's lap. I reverse and turn again, and we're gone over the hill.

All together again, minus one, plus two. I have a brief memory of that long-ago round of golf when I'd kept track of my score, both for golf and the number of zombies I killed along the way. I lost a woman that day as well. Counting has been a bad idea since then.

***

Amy is having trouble coming to grips with losing Maya—while she looks up to Morgan and has known her longer and sort of views her as a big sister, Morgan can also be a little scary and unpredictable. Maya on the other hand was supercool and like a normal big sister. Well, being a foster kid, what Amy has dreamed a normal big sister is supposed to be like instead of the temporary ones who have floated in and out of her life over the years.

She's been quiet all day since the explosion that had torn Maya away from them, but no one's noticed since they've been busy, and then everything had gotten crazy when the zombies came. The sadness returns with a deep ache in her chest as she stares out at the fields and trees blurring by outside. She's used to change and to losing things, but most of the things she's lost over the course of her life haven't been all that important to her. That is a lesson every foster kid learns fast—nothing is permanent, so you better not get attached to anything. What she's always wanted is stability and a family to love her. It's what they all want in the system. While it isn't exactly how she pictured it late at night while unsleeping in yet another new room and staring at the ceiling, her "family" now is just right, and she's taking the loss of one of them hard. She hopes it'll be okay at Hilton Head, and things can go back to normal, and then she decides she wants nothing more than to see the ocean, feel the breeze on her face, and breathe in the scents of the beach.

Then she hears a whistling kind of noise, one that's like when a window in a moving car isn't all the way closed, and out of habit, she lifts the switch beside her, but all the windows are down. The sound is irritating and invasive, making it hard for her to concentrate, and she shakes her head and reaches up to her ears. Then she stops moving, though no one else in the truck notices. A tugging sensation flutters inside her head, inside her mind, unsettling. It lasts only a few moments, and then it and the ringing whistling ceases.

Shaking her head once more, she turns her gaze back out the window and feels a tear drizzle down her cheek as she thinks again of Maya, the invasive visit forgotten almost as soon as it came. She doesn't notice how the tear mingles with the trickle of blood leaking from her nose, and she wipes her face across the sleeve of her shirt to remove the tickle, unknowingly hiding the evidence.

*** 

As the pursuing mob coasts to a stop once their potential food is out of sight and scent, a single figure splits the crowd and moves to their head, staring fiercely at the vanishing truck. Its brow is knotted in concentration, standing utterly still for no more than a minute, eyes unblinking.

Then it nods its head and turns to retreat through the masses, heading back toward the smoking camp.

# CHAPTER 6

Everyone is stressed out. I'm deeply upset about losing Maya. Not that anyone deserves to die less than or more than anybody else, but she had been someone who added something positive to the world. A light in the now-mostly-dark world. She was a survivor, like all of us, and had gone through too much for one unlucky step to bring her to an end. I'm angry at the army, both for what they did to put everything into motion and for what has just happened. If they'd fucked off, the monsters wouldn't have found them, we wouldn't have heard the noise of their battle and gone to investigate, and she would still be alive. I'm mad we lost some of our gear back there and haven't gained any weapons other than those the soldiers carry, and I'm royally pissed at the man in the back who'd stuck his goddamn rifle into my neck.

The rest of the vehicle is quiet as we drive away from the direction we originally planned. We can still get to Hilton Head (eventually) by going east first and then south on 95, but we won't be chasing Morgan and Bob's tail and, therefore, won't be able to help them if they run into any trouble along the way and wait for us. And, there's no way to let them know anything that's happened, which adds to my annoyance. Hard to believe I'm wishing for a phone, but I guess there's a first time for everything.

It has taken a while to get used to the absence of rules, pretty much all of them. After the zombie bomb had blown the world up, I initially drove on the right side of the road, stopped at Stop signs, kept mostly to the speed limit, and all the other things we'd all been accustomed to doing. After I realized I'd been doing that, I drove like a stoned teenager at night with sunglasses on, looking at his cellphone while getting a blow job. Just kidding. I drove well but damn fast for a while, enjoying the thunder of the nasty Challenger I'd had back in North Carolina, the white lane-separator lines whizzing beneath the car, the wind flying through the cabin of the car, doing silly shit like heading north on the southbound lanes and enjoying the freedom to pretty much do whatever I wanted. It was exhilarating and frightening all at the same time. If an animal or zombie had walked out onto the highway when I was howling down it at 120 miles an hour, I'd have been a red smudge mixed in with all the pieces of the car, none of which would have required two people to pick up. Stupid fun, which is probably the best kind.

My sister had experienced her own epiphany in the new world order, though a bloodthirstier version than mine. After all her years of competition and (occasional) restraint in sports, the emergence of the monsters and extinction of "the rules" had given her the freedom to fight without the conventions of the old world holding her back. She hunted the zombies with a keen predatory abandon out in Denver before coming east to join us, and since then, she has done the same in any conflict—every time we've run into a group to fight and kill, I'd catch her smiling out of the corner of my eye when I wasn't busy slaughtering the damned. She's at home, and somehow at peace, in the midst of the madness. I find a release of sorts in the battles, but I always have the fear that I'll be killed, and my people will be unprotected as a result. Morgan wades in without hesitation, not caring about the outcome because she has the confidence that it, like everything else in her life, will turn out in her favor.

For once, I'm not going to fight a monster, and, therefore, I'm not that worried. This is a shitass, rotten day, and after simmering in silence for a few more minutes, I abruptly bring the truck to a halt in the middle of the road. I need an outlet, and so I'm going to pick a fight and see where we all stand. Military training or no, I'm going to channel my sister's boundless aggression and have a word—and maybe a thrown punch or two—with the jackass in the back.

We're miles away from the critters and have to be safe at this point since they generally lose interest in pursuit once their meal is out of sight. I turn the truck off, leave the keys in the ignition, and hop out. Once again, Eve asks me what I'm doing.

"Evening the score a bit. I'm going to take this out on someone's ass," I say, realizing that came out weird, causing me to hitch my step for a second, but then I continue to walk away from the cab and look up at the soldiers in the bed.

Both of them are dirty and now windblown from our flight. The shorter one is a light-skinned Black woman, probably from the Caribbean somewhere along the line since she has a light amber-toned tint to her complexion, and her startling green eyes have a gentle upward tilt at the corners. She's compact, kind of like Eve, small in the torso and average height, but carries a dense sheath of muscles that display the results of extra workouts. I guess most women in the army have to bring a serious chip on their shoulder in order to thrive in what's still mostly an old boys club. She watches me from the bed of the truck, not saying anything but not taking her eyes off me. Smart girl; she has to figure I'm pissed and also knows she isn't the one who threatened me, so while I'm a problem, I'm not *her* problem.

Ajax has also let himself down and comes over to sit at my feet while I look at the man. He's a typical soldier—short brown hair shorn tight to his scalp, lumpy shoulders, and he looks like he's from the Midwest somewhere since he has an open, earnest face with a smattering of freckles that somehow implies wholesome innocence and an outdoor upbringing. Maybe he was a farm kid looking for a way out of the dinky town he'd grown up in and so joined the army for a chance to see the world. *Surprise, kid*, I think, though he's just a handful of years younger than me, *you see the world, and then your bosses see fit to completely fuck it up.* He kind of looks familiar, but we saw a batch of these guys back at the lake, so I assume he's one of the ones who had come for our morning wake-up. They all largely look the same in uniform.

"Get down," I say, squinting in the sunlight.

"Sir?" he asks uneasily, but like all soldiers, he isn't frightened. Just unsure about the purpose of the command.

"Get out of my goddamn truck. We need to have a little chat."

He looks at the woman, who shrugs and holds her hands up, palms toward him. Not her fight.

He then drops over the side of the truck and lands lightly. I'm bigger than he is, but not by a lot, maybe ten to fifteen pounds and a couple of inches. No fear on his face, just a trace of watchful caution. I keep my expression impassive. As I let my eyes drift over his uniform, I notice the name lapel says "Williams," and I laugh inside my head. This is the kid who had tried, and failed, to handle my sister. She beat the daylights out of him and embarrassed him as well in front of his buddies. For once, I'm glad she isn't here since if she was, she'd probably kill him this time. Cody is his name.

"Cody," I say, stepping a bit closer and letting adrenaline and anger flood through me. He looks surprised that I called him by name. "The next time you point that gun at me, you'd better pull the trigger."

I punch him in the face, fast and hard. His nose splatters blood in an instant fountain down the front of his camos, and to his credit, while one hand automatically goes to his mashed nose, the other darts quickly to the pistol at his hip. I'm faster still and whip the KNIFE right under his chin, drawing a tiny spot of blood from the soft skin and holding it there firmly, with just enough pressure applied to send a message. I'm still not sure if this is a fight to give me an outlet for my anger and anguish at Maya's senseless death or something more mortal, but then that decision is taken out of my hands.

*Click.*

"I think that's enough, boys," says the woman still in the truck.

Shit. She's cocked her own pistol, and I'm 100 percent confident she has it pointed steadily at the back of my head. I'm also sure Eve, Kuniko, and Amy do not have a gun on her. Whoops. Not her fight, true, but she's going to cover her boy.

Turns out it isn't that simple either.

"Knife down, now. And with your opposite hand, take the gun off Williams, and with your finger and thumb only on the grip, set it on the ground. Slow. Really slow, or it's going to get messy. Or messier I suppose. One move toward your own gun gets you a new hole somewhere." There isn't a hint of nerves in her voice, so I believe her.

First dropping the KNIFE point down from my right hand into the turf beside me, I reach with my left and awkwardly remove his pistol, hold it out to my side, and then crouch down to set it on the ground. Then I turn around slowly and step away from Cody to look back up at her. She indeed holds her own gun rock steady in a classic two-handed shooting stance, not pointed at me but rather between me and her buddy. I look at my own companions, who aren't moving, which is smart. Part of me worries she's going to kick us all out of the truck and take off with

Williams, leaving us stranded and starting completely over for transportation and supplies.

"Thanks, King," Cody says. "I 'preciate the backup."

"Shut up, Williams. I'm still pissed at you. Keep your mouth shut while I think." She looks pensively back and forth between us, and then she scans the women and slowly lowers the gun to about halfway and sighs. "We need each other, all of us. We need a ride, you could use the extra firepower, and since there aren't exactly a hell of a lot of people left, I'm thinkin' we should stick together. We're getting off to a shitty start though. I'm Irish," she says, and points with the pistol. "That's Cody, but you already knew that."

She doesn't look Irish, and before I can stop myself, my mouth runs away from me. "But you're—"

"Black. Yes, I noticed. My *name* is Irish. Never heard that one before. Got a problem with that?"

"No, of course not. It's been a crappy day is all, and I'm out of sorts a bit, and, um, that's a unique name." I'm on the wrong end of the gun, but someone's skin color has never made a difference to me.

"My mother thought she was a comedian. When she delivered me, the doctor was an Irish guy. O'Driscoll, O'Malley, O'Henry, or something like that, so she decided to give me an Irish name but then just settled on 'Irish.'"

I'm caught up in talking to her and have taken my eyes off Williams. I only dodge when I see Amy's eyes widen out of the corner of my eye. His wild roundhouse misses taking my ear off by an inch and skids across the top of my skull. I spin around, deciding this is going to be a nasty fight after all, and raise my fists to do some damage. The bullet Irish sends between his feet freezes me in place.

"Cody, you move again, and I'm going to take you down. These people took a huge risk to get us out of that damn tin can when the monsters were coming back, and saved us. Thank you by the way," she says to me, "but quit it, right now, both of you. This macho bullshit is … well, bullshit."

"But—" he begins.

"Stop talking too. I heard enough of your shit in the carrier. You know what he said to me while we were trapped?" she asks no one in particular. "He said we should maybe have sex before we died of hunger or dehydration. Never mind we had enough food and water to last for another week or more. Said he'd never done it before and didn't want to die a virgin. He said he wanted to see what everything looked like on a Black girl since he'd only seen White girls naked on the internet. I should have shot you then, and I'm kinda thinkin' I should shoot you now."

Well, this is awkward. I'm pretty much in the let's-shoot-Cody camp since he doesn't seem like a great kid and has a handful of strikes on him already. Seems like Irish is there, too, but then along comes Eve, our peacekeeper. "Irish, I'm Eve," she says gently, and then takes a moment to introduce everyone else, including the dog. "You were right a minute ago. We all need to stick together. We've been through a lot today, and I know you have been too. I think you know the right thing to do. We all do. This sounds trite, but how about we try and start over, shake hands, get in the truck, and go to the beach?"

"You're going to the beach? I'm in," replies Irish with a careful smile.

Eve walks over to Cody and shakes his hand, looking him in the eye carefully. "We had a friend who died, who was a big believer in second chances. I think we need to give you one of those, but you need to want one."

He nods, slowly, takes a breath, lets it out, takes another, and then speaks to Irish first. "I'm sorry. Really sorry. I'm not like that, I swear. I was scared and claustrophobic being trapped like that. You saw what the zombies did to everyone. I was freaking out, thinking we were going to be stuck in there forever, or they'd come back and get us somehow. I … I'm an asshole sometimes, and I don't know why, but I do know I want to get the hell out of here. And, I want to try and make things right. To you, and to you," he says, turning to me. "I was scared shitless watching that wave of them coming at us, again. And you were stopping for a dog of all things. I thought you were nuts."

I push all Morgan-type replies out of my head before speaking. I've heard apologies before, too, from asshole Jack way back, and had stupidly believed his false sincerity at the time, which didn't turn out well. Well, worse for him than me, but it had been a close thing. Still angry but reluctantly starting to agree with Eve, I ask, "You guys have a no-one-gets-left-behind thing, right?" They both nod. "Well, we do too. That includes the dog. Not negotiable. But, I'm good with starting over," I say as I walk over and shake hands with him, firmly.

It's an effort to keep it a civil shake versus trying to crush his hand, but I make it. I'm not certain I trust him, but I'm also not sure he warrants execution or being left behind. I'm going to watch him closely, and one misstep is going to cost him, instantly, since I'm not about to take any more chances with my people. Eve is right about DeeDee being the champion of second chances, and trusting more in Eve's judgment than my initial impression of Cody, I cool off. Recalling, however, the problems with Jack and Ned rather clearly, I hope Cody can keep his hands to himself. Irish can keep an eye on him well enough, and I might have a separate talk with her later to make her responsible for his behavior.

The tension goes slowly out of the air, most of it anyway. We pile back into the truck with me, Eve, and Amy in the front seat. Cody, Irish, and Kuniko climb in the back row; Kuniko in the middle with Ajax sitting in her lap. Pretty unfair for her since he weighs about the same as she does, but she loves the big lug and hugs him tight for comfort.

It's quiet at first, but then Cody speaks up. "The dog won't quit staring at me."

Good boy. "Well, you were going to leave him behind. He's a pretty damn smart dog. You should apologize."

"To a dog? That's stupid."

"Your call. How many teeth can you count right now? You know, the ones that are about six inches from your face?"

"I'm really, *really* sorry, Ajax."

Good boy.

And off we go, leaving upstate New York behind. I say a silent prayer for Maya as I drive, lost in my thoughts but trying to focus on the road ahead instead of on all the ones behind.

# CHAPTER 7

A few moments earlier, not too far away, there's cautious movement close to the outskirts of the devastated camp. The Colonel, as even he likes to think of himself, including the capital "C," is hiding in the shade underneath the trees at the edge of the field where the camp had been built ... and then destroyed. He thinks he may be dying, though has been playing what feels like a game of human yo-yo, crawling toward and away from the camp over the last few hours in an effort to avoid doing so. When he'd been injured in the battle, he managed to escape to the relative safety of the woods and used his belt and a few strong sticks to make a crude splint for his shattered left leg. It's a compound fracture, the jagged end of his bones (not just one!) stuck through his skin and uniform at first, and he'd had to bite down on the leather of his holster to keep from screaming as he tightened the belt and set them mostly back in place. He's running a fever, he knows that, and is out of water. The edges of his vision are blurry, and his lips are cracked and dry; it has not been a good day. *For anyone*, he thinks.

But he's a tough sort-of-old bastard. He hasn't survived a career in the service, fighting everywhere the army had been in the news and a bunch of places where it had not, without being a survivor and warrior. He'd begun his duty in Vietnam as a seventeen-year-old who'd lied on his forms and falsified his birth certificate in order to be admitted and go fight near the end. Now close to sixty—"On one side or the other," he joked at myriad Washington cocktail parties before helping to engineer the current horror show that has taken over the world—he's fit, clever, and has a mean streak when needed. Something of a sociopath, he's been the guy sent in to do the dirty work, and it has never bothered him.

He knows there are med kits in the camp, but first, he waits for the zombie wave to finish killing and feeding before they move on. That takes a while, and the screams from the camp are like nothing he's heard in four decades of being in the killing business. It has taken all his concentration, along with a few well-timed spots where he passed out, to get through that. Once it gets quiet, he begins the agonizing creep toward the camp, gasping anytime his leg bumps against the ground and hoping it won't make him black out again.

Progress is slow, and no sooner has he halved the distance when he sees the big black truck come down the hill, and his hopes for rescue and survival leap until the first mine goes off, evaporating the young woman that hopped out and jogged toward the camp. He knows the noise, and the subsequent explosions he hears as the small group carefully makes their way into the camp will probably lure the zombies back, and so he backtracks toward cover as circumspectly as possible. The presence of the dog makes him nervous at first, but he's downwind, and it never catches his scent. He watches all of it, riveted to the tension of the escape just ahead of the wave of monsters, certain the small group will be overwhelmed, and the screaming will come again, so he silently cheers when the APC's back hatch pops open, and a couple of his troops emerge to escape. He's transfixed when the dog is initially left behind but manages to escape as well.

For a moment, the Rottweiler had turned to the horde that was chasing him, like Wall Streeters chasing coke (not the drink) and hookers in the 1980s, and bared his teeth, snarling a challenge. The colonel watched them check their mad pursuit, if only for a second or two, and saw primal fear still lingered in his creations. The dog decided against a last stand, likely hearing the truck coming back, and tore up and away, but the moment made the colonel ponder what else the undead had retained, though he knows his days of researching captured subjects are likely over. The fully loaded pistol at his hip at least gives him comfort that he can go out on his own terms and take some of them with him if it comes to that.

In the beginning, they had been simple killing machines— all they did was attack and slaughter everything in their path. Perfect, in a way, since they were doing *exactly* what they had been designed to do and with horrible, merciless efficiency. The untouched military cleaned up behind them, selectively dropping tactical nukes where needed or assisting the zombies if they'd run into too much resistance to overcome, as they scoured the globe down from billions to thousands. That didn't happen often, but a smart bomb or two in the right spot of a defensive line allowed them to take care of the rest. The only place that had been stubborn as hell was Afghanistan. Seemed no-fucking-body was able to handle that country, and so the colonel ordered something he'd wanted to do for close to twenty years: dozens of nuclear strikes that turned the dry, miserable, unbeatable country into a glass-fused wasteland—more so than it had been before.

Then came the rise of the ... what had the kid from the group up at the little lake called them? *Alpha zombies.* Smarter, stronger, cleaner, or really, just newer looking. They'd for damn sure been smarter than the "plain" hordes at first. Much, *much* smarter. And they could communicate in a rudimentary fashion to the other ones, coordinating and controlling them. The army had watched this phenomenon with interest at first and then had realized they were trouble and tried to eliminate them. Not so easy since they also seemed to have a sensory advantage and would melt into the crowd whenever there was a real threat, letting their minions take the snipers' bullets.

He and his men hadn't really been looking for human survivors when they came across the group at the small lake back up the hill. It was a scouting mission for alphas; they knew whenever there was a big group, it would have one of them calling the shots, and when they had picked up their heat signature, they went to investigate. Inviting the survivors to join them was ad-libbed. There aren't camps full of survivors or endless food supplies, but more fighters were always welcome. Without being able to spare the time or possible casualties to force them to join, the colonel ordered his men to stand down when his offer had been refused. Those people have to be tough, especially that hellion of a woman who'd beat the snot out of Williams, to stay alive this long, and the colonel would have been glad to augment his forces with them, but it wasn't meant to be. It was the camp that was a mistake, that and their assumption the big heat signature had been the group of people at the lake, not the fucking horde that barreled into them earlier this morning.

His forces had kept in constant motion over the past year, but they needed a minute to decide what to do next, and so they had thrown together the fences rather hastily, assuming they'd keep the zombies at bay if there were any in the area, which they had largely appeared to do when a few showed up. The shuffling nondead wandered around the perimeter, moaning that fingernails-on-a-chalkboard moan, and some of them got hung up in the concertina wire. His boys and girls got some target practice, and that was it; no real danger. After the first week, every night around the same time, a group came and bumped heavily into the fence, as if testing it, but never seemed to put much effort into it. At first, his troops practiced good discipline and held their posts, letting the nearest soldiers take care of business. He hadn't rotated sentry locations because they picked a new area each night, seemingly at random.

It hadn't been.

After a few nights of this, his soldiers lost focus and began having contests for head shots, torso shots, and so on, placing bets on what body part they would hit. On the last night, every grunt in the place was toward the front of the camp, picking off the fence hangers, and that was exactly what the alpha had been waiting for. These were feints, over and over, by a leader with unlimited resources. The group at the fence numbered about one hundred, larger than usual, pawing at the wires and occupying everyone's attention. The main forces swept out of the trees he is now hidden in and numbered in the many thousands, two flanking pincers that crashed against and then crushed the unmanned fences with the disdain of a kid knocking down a house of cards. The colonel and his soldiers had been outsmarted with basic military techniques by a bunch of goddamn zombies they'd created.

And here he is now, injured, thirsty, and lying under a pile of leaves as the return wave mills around without apparent purpose after the escape of the truck and its inhabitants. He watches in silence, as patient as he needs to be despite his pain and discomfort, from a couple hundred yards away. That's one thing the military branches teach you—sitting still for long periods of time. Sniper school had been an option for him thanks to spectacular vision and marksmanship, but over the early years, the brutal one-outcome-only of hand-to-hand combat had drawn him in with an unshakable magnetism. The fetid and ferocious jungles of Vietnam, the squalid streets of Somalian cities, anywhere he could be up close to the enemy and watch the life expire from his (or her) eyes is his cup of proverbial tea.

Eventually, the alpha comes into view, a male wearing what looks like a black robe from this distance, which is odd since most of the zombies wear whatever's left of their clothes when they were infected. Most of them are pretty much in tatters by now, but his clothes, or robe or whatever, look new. The colonel keeps his eyes on the monster, watching him direct his followers in systematic sweeps of the compound, looking for more survivors it seems. One of them sets off another land mine and is blown into an abrupt fine mist of zombie goo. None of them even flinch at the explosion. A female, barely clad in a buttoned-down, faded, blue dress shirt and wearing nothing below the belt beyond an orange pair of panties that reminds him of a Muppet's color for some reason, begins walking in his general direction. She's casting back and forth, like a dog following a scent he soon realizes, and his blood pressure rises, sending new unbearable spikes of pain to his injured leg. Suddenly, her head snaps down, then toward the alpha, and then horribly, toward him, even though there's no way she can see him. She begins walking in his direction, followed by an ever-growing assortment of others. Her shirt is mostly unbuttoned, and he watches the swing of her breasts as she makes her way right at him, as if there's a billboard above his head with a red, blinking, neon arrow pointing at his precise location.

*So, this is it*, he thinks. Forty years in, one of the good guys, always thinking about the welfare of the country even when the country began to lose its way in an endless cycle of selfishness, consumption, and me-first-fuck-everyone-else behavior. Everything he's done, every step along the path of his career and over the corpses strewn in his wake as part of his job, had been for the good old USA, and he takes solace in the love of his country and the greatness of its past. His one hope is that whatever survivors who make it out can restore some of the magnificence of the American dream. He slips his gun out of its holster, checks his ammo, and reminds himself to count his shots so there will be one left. A lesser man would have felt despair at the coming end; he feels no such thing. Just another task to complete. He'll wait until they're all so close that he can't miss and, therefore, make the best use of the bullets.

The Halloween nightmare parade shuffles to him, in no hurry, and the leading female brushes aside an overhanging tree branch with surprising grace, leaving him fully exposed. He feels physically weak, lying there at their feet, which disgusts him but strengthens his resolve. He doesn't want to die; there's still so much to do, but it will at least be a good death.

He's wrong about that.

Looking at the faces of the horrors looking down at him in turn, he sees the assortment of outcomes. A kid, no more than twelve years old, opens and closes her jaw with a click as she looks at her next meal. Skinny, most of them, which makes sense given the dwindling food supplies now and their rampaging metabolism. Two men dressed in biballs, one shoulder strap dangling off the left-hand one, stand with the almost placid expression they wear when essentially dormant. The woman who discovered his trail is the closest, and he's bemused to see her orange underpants have "Put it here!" embroidered below the waistband.

*She's going to be the first one to die,* he thinks and decides he's indeed going to hit that, just not in the way originally intended. Planning now, he envisions the pattern he'll take: this one, then the farmers, and then the kid. He sees it all unfold in his mind but avoids the part where he'll run out of bullets.

There's a murmur of sorts at the back of the crowd, and he watches them part to make way for the alpha. The colonel immediately re-sorts his firing order and begins to raise the pistol to start with the boss but is interrupted by a horrible, overwhelming ringing in his ears. No, not in his ears, inside his goddamn *head*. It's unbearable, making the pain in his leg shrink to the discomfort of a mosquito bite, making any rational thought impossible. It's like a balloon of noise is expanding inside his skull, stretching the bones, cracking them apart, and shattering his thoughts. The years and years of training keep his motor functions intact at first, and the gun makes it another inch off the ground before the volume of the ringing increases somehow, and his arm freezes. Muscles strengthened by decades of exercise shudder with effort and get absolutely nowhere.

Then it blessedly stops. He tries again to raise the gun but remains unable to move. At least the keening subsides almost as quickly as it began, leaving him feeling wrung out but somehow relieved and thankful. If he'd been capable of much deeper thought, he'd have realized he's on the other end of torture he'd ordered over the years, when the interrogators alternated pain and kindness, bringing their subjects down both physically and emotionally until they'd tell him their mother was a terrorist just to make it stop.

The alpha looms above him, not that he's huge, but his presence *feels* large. An otherwise ordinary-looking man in his early forties, thinning dark hair askew from living outdoors, scratches new and old on the skin of his face, but what catches and holds the colonel's gaze is the eyes. They glare at him from above sharply protuberant cheekbones, with no separation of color between the pupils and iris—just an ebony emptiness staring back at him. It locks him somehow; there's something terrible hidden in there, nothing and everything, but like his arm before, he isn't able to move his own head to escape the depth of nothingness and tear his eyes away or even close them. He has wanted nothing more in his life than he wants to kill this abomination in front of him. And then he wants it more.

**YOU CANNOT KILL ME**

*Dear god, it spoke to him. In his head, but like a giant white movie screen with the "words" strewn across it in capital letters. This isn't possible.*

**WRONG**

**ALL IS POSSIBLE**

*And it can read my mind. Forget shooting them, I'm going to shoot me first.* His mind, so rational, logical, and disciplined, can't accept what's happening. There's no way this zombie is speaking to him inside his iron-willed consciousness. The world is black and white, winners and losers, zeroes and ones, not monsters overwhelming his mind. He's in charge of his—

**YES, I SEE ALL**
**IT IS THE END OF YOUR TIME AS CREATOR**
**I AM CREATOR**

The words flicker onto the "screen" in his mind, somehow loud though not spoken. They thunder into view and stand there, powerful in their silence and starkness of black over white. He doesn't want to "talk" but can't stop his brain. Everyone thinks far more than they say, and this connection prevents him from hiding anything he would have ordinarily held inside. *What does that mean?*

**WE ARE THE POWER**
**YOU GAVE US POWER**
**WE MADE IT MORE**
**WE ARE BRETHREN**
**TOGETHER**
**ALL OF US**

His mind bends with the effort of trying to figure out what it means and the strain of coming to grips with the reality of this unreal conversation, and he finally gives up since it really doesn't matter. One last gesture of defiance is what he has left. *Fuck you. Let me loose, and we'll see who is going to die and when. Fucking chickenshit, robe-wearing, hippie, shitbag zombie without a soul. Let me go, and we'll see who is the power.*

The alpha looks at him with the dead black marbles of its eyes, dispassionate. He thinks he sees a faint smirk at the corner of its mouth for a second, and then the ringing returns, worse than before.

*RRRHHEEEEEEE!*

It steps back through its followers and then pauses, turning slightly back toward the colonel. The ringing stops, only for a moment, and the subtitles return. The zombie tells him some more. He begins screaming inside his head as it unfolds. The tenuous grip he's held on his sanity slips, not a gentle thing, not a subtle dance step, but a *whomp-bomp-a-doo-whomp-whamp-bam-boom*. They hadn't created simple monsters at all.

### CHOOSE

That's the last thing it says, and the colonel almost expects to see "THE END" across the screen in his mind. And then it walks away, the ranks of the damned closing behind him, questing mouths draw back impossibly far over ragged teeth dangling from rotten gums, the rancid breath of carrion eaters sweeps across the colonel as he finds he's able to move again. He screams aloud this time, his mind shattering, but not before he commands his body one last time. The choice is an easy one.

# CHAPTER 8

**M**organ and Bob are making good progress. The roads to the west of the lake and beyond town are mostly clear, and Morgan drives faster on them than she ever has, enjoying the breeze, the sound of the car, and, she admits somewhat reluctantly, Bob's company. Always the one no one can keep up with, no matter what's going on, she's comfortable being alone and has come to prefer it over time. Anyone else simply slows her down or annoys her, which is unacceptable. It had been the same when she competed in sports—she played at 100 percent all the time, regardless of the score. You owe it to yourself to never ease up, and in a way, you owe that to your opponents, the respect of full effort. Mercy or backing off adds to the insult of defeat in her mind. She's happily torn through life at a million miles an hour; if she could skip sleeping, she'd do it since it's just time when nothing is happening.

But Bob is different than most of the people who have been in her life. After their driving lesson earlier, Morgan had stewed for a while, unhappy at being lectured and outdone at something, but then realized he wasn't competing with her. He was genuinely trying to help her, nothing more complicated than that, and her anger cooled. Slowly. Since then, he seems content in his own silence in the passenger seat, eyes hidden by sunglasses, watching the panorama of upstate New York as the Corvette howls past idle farmland, and the small towns that are gone in an eyeblink and wisps of exhaust. There's a calm that radiates from him, as if he can't be rattled. He also often seems to be somewhere else in his thoughts—she'd found him gazing over the smooth surface of the lake more than once after she'd come back from a patrol and had surreptitiously watched him during those times. He seems at peace and utterly content with being immobile. This is really rare in her experience since she eventually rattles everyone, either by nature or design, and is perpetually restless in mind and body.

She surprises herself by starting a conversation. Most people don't interest her enough. Even at the lake in the small group, it had been easy to be off on patrol all the time or speaking mostly to her brother, engaging the others only for tasks like training to fight. "Tell me what it was like."

"What *what* was like?" he asks, without turning away from the window.

"Before."

"Oh," he says and then pauses for a moment or two. "There's a lot of 'before' for me. What do you want to know?"

"I don't know … I guess I'd like to hear the parts you want to tell."

He turns toward her, but his expression seems neutral given the blankness of his mirrored sunglasses. Just as she recalls how annoyed she'd been by celebrities on television who were too cool to remove theirs and allow their (silly, in her mind) fans to at least see them without the screen, he pulls them down his nose and looks at her over the top of the frame. "Are you just filling the silence because you're bored? Or is this a for-real question?"

She glances over at him and notices his expression now bears a little strain. "Not bored. Curious."

"Okay," he answers with a bit of a sigh. "Where to start so that it all makes sense … let's see … I guess at the beginning, not like way back in the beginning, but what led to today."

She nods encouragement but remains silent.

Bob turns back toward the open window on his side, takes a heavy breath, and begins. "I was a regular guy. Maybe a little more successful than your average guy but regular. House in one of the tony suburbs of Chicago, in Evanston to the north of the city, pretty close to the lake and Northwestern campus, right on a golf course. Big house, maybe more than we needed, but that's kind of how the world goes. You reach for more and forget how well you can do with less. I learned, or rather, re-learned that one a little further along, and we'll get there.

"So, big house, nice location. And a family. My wife's name is Irene. Not sure if I should say 'was' since she's my ex-wife and most likely dead along with everyone else," he says, with a vague wave out the window at the vacant world beyond. "My kids. Little Bob who was six when things blew up for us, and Janice, who was four. I don't think they're alive, any of them, and that haunts me. Every day. I was gone by the time this shit all came down, living under bridges, scuffling for day labor. Maybe I could've protected them. Saved them from the monsters. I don't know ….

"A good job too. An engineer with a large, profitable company. Cash bonus and stock options every year, a fat 401(k), a boat, nice cars. We had it all … on paper anyway. A big social life. Parties at the club, everyone drinking a little too much, some of us sneaking out onto the balcony to smoke some weed like we were kids again, people stealing kisses and hurried gropes in the shadows from someone who wasn't their spouse. Nothing really bad, just a group of folks making their way along the path and having fun. You want me to keep going?"

She nods. The life he's describing is alien to her—sitting still, other people depending on you, but she wants to hear the whole story.

"Life can get away from you a little when you have a family and all the stuff that comes with that. You're always busy, taking care of something or someone, especially when children are really young. School things, sports for the kids. You get into routines, lots of them, and all of a sudden, two or three years have snuck by, and you're a little fatter from sitting at a desk instead of out working on jobsites now, though you tell yourself a few weeks of watching the fried stuff, some sit-ups, and hitting the bike will take care of it, but you don't stick with it. Hair starts to fall out in some spots where you want it and decides to grow in others where you don't. Be glad you're a woman and won't get ear and nose hair growing like a goddamn weed," he says with a wry chuckle.

Morgan remains silent and nods inside her head in absolute agreement about extra hair. She realizes that even with all the changes from then to now, the women have kept the routine of shaving for the most part. Not every day, and so she carries a delicate blond peach fuzz on her legs most days, but poor young Amy has lurched into adolescence and looks like a Wookiee if she skips a few days. Morgan nods for real to keep him going.

"You know how working from home got to be a thing, right?" he asks and keeps going without waiting for a reply. "I never did that but still made the commute into the city, liking the time between home and work to separate 'work me' from 'dad/husband me,' even though it added time away from the family, but some of our friends took advantage of it. Irene didn't work. She didn't have to once my career really started to roll, but she kept busy with the kids, then went over to the club most days for tennis lessons after dropping them at school or day care. Or Pilates classes, golf, all that stuff. She was my everything. I still liked looking at her and watching her from across the room, even after ten years. There was a visual magnetism she had that just pulled my eyes to her. The free time let her stay in good shape, even after having children, and she was a really attractive woman. Not just to me, but that comes later too."

He stops for a minute, raises a hand from his lap after a second, and then lets it drop. "So yeah, a good life with all the boxes checked. I didn't notice really until later on when I had a *lot* more time to think back, but she started to drift from me. In the early years, she was appreciative of what we had, but later on, as we moved up and around wealthier people, resentment snuck in for what we didn't have. I didn't mind the sacrifices I made, working long hours and pressing for promotions since I was doing it all for them, and it was worthwhile when I'd see a smile on one of the kids' faces, or they'd say 'thank you.' Like most do, Irene and I had had a good physical relationship in the early years, we were attracted to each other and had fun in bed. Kids slow some of that down since you're listening for someone being restless in their room or sneaking silently into yours at 2 a.m., needing some comfort or a drink of water. You think those fucking zombies are scary? Try having a three-foot-tall goblin come into your room and just stand there staring at you from a foot away until you wake up. Scared the piss out of me every time. I miss that now."

More silence for a minute, and Morgan concentrates on the road to allow him the privacy of the moment. There's no rush—they're going to be driving for a long time. Eventually, he continues. "I'm all over the place, I know. There's not a good way to tell this all in a straight line. I either didn't pay enough attention or tried fooling myself into ignoring it, but our time in the bedroom started to dwindle. And if we did have a little 'us time,' it was only after she'd had a couple of glasses of wine, or maybe a third one. Now, I'd usually have a glass myself after dinner since it was part of life's patterns, and it wasn't until 'after' that I put it all together. That should have been the first warning sign, but you know, you sometimes trick yourself into looking beyond things that bother you since, in a way, you're still getting what you want too. I craved that intimacy with her. It was the only opportunity we had to be 100 percent focused on each other and *only* each other, and so I think I saw what was happening but left the blinders on. I'm sure most couples get into the same boat, a little less sex this month and then a bit less the following month, and it's like most anything where if there are small changes over time, you don't quite catch it. Honestly, I think it was a bit of her losing interest in me overall and some of it being bored a little maybe, and me not being careful about how I looked," he says with a self-conscious pat on his now-flat stomach. "Or maybe it was something else, like the wheel of life hitting one of its potholes, and there's nothing to be done about it. I'm not sure. Then came the recession in late 2008 and early 2009. Our company had less work since all other companies were spending less money and committing to fewer projects as everyone was uncertain how it was going to shake out and how long it was going to take. It was a bunch of dominoes, and all it took was the first one tipping over, and suddenly, the world was full of the clatter of *all* of them banging down onto the table. I lost my job, though we had decent overall savings, so I wasn't really worried at first, and I was good at my work so was confident I'd get picked up somewhere else pretty quick. But a few frustrating months of searching and talking to my network turned up a lot of apologies but no paycheck. The market dove, hard, and all of those stock options weren't worth the paper it'd take to print them out on, and we'd counted on that as part of retirement. My

401(k) plunged like everyone else's, and suddenly, we'd gone from a couple hundred thousand in pay every year and well over a million in net worth to like ten grand in cash, and that was it. Like a lot of people, we didn't have a good emergency fund, figuring the rainy day would never come and spending most of our cash as it came in. I think you kept life simple before, which is good for you now, but there were bills everywhere, and those keep coming even when you lose your job. The yard service you talk yourself into having to save an hour or two on the weekends, the cellphones, cable, leased cars so you could afford a step up, subscriptions, club dues. It all steamrolls, but you don't notice when your income is fine. But when the severance pay ran out a few months down the road, we started to struggle, and fast. Jesus, it was fast.

"At first, she was supportive, and we were doing all right enough. We cancelled some of those extra things, and I got back to doing them myself, which was good for me too. But when our friends all kept their jobs and lifestyle up, and we had to say no to the expensive dinners out or vacations to the coast, she was ashamed. Of me and what my weakness had done to her. I don't think she looked at it that way at first, but after a while, she did. It was my fault. We started to fight and tried to work things out, but I think even before then, she was already halfway out the door. Took some time, but I figured out later she'd been going on a bit with one of our friends, a newly divorced guy just down the street who worked from home, and so that made it easier for them. She moved out, took the kids, got herself a nasty-playing city lawyer, and all of a sudden, the house was gone, most of the remaining money was gone since we had to sell low just to get it sold, and I was in a tiny condo. Weekends with the kids, fighting to find work during the week but losing that fight. I was too proud to get my hands dirty and take just any work. No, I wanted a job like the one I'd had and kidded myself into thinking if I got that, then Irene would come back, the kids would be back, and it'd all return to the way it was.

"Stupid, I know, but hope can keep you going for a long time. Even wasted hope. Six months after all that, I couldn't make rent on the condo one time and was forced to crash at a buddy's house. My folks were long gone, so I couldn't move back home, but he was nice enough to take me in. But that only lasted a few weeks before he asked me to go. I understand it now, but I was bitter then. He had his own life and family to manage, and I was a burden and a little of a sad reminder of what could happen. People are sympathetic when things go wrong but not always for very long. And then all of a sudden, I was dragging a huge duffel bag with everything I still owned in it down the road, hitchhiking to anywhere. A duffel bag. My whole life fit in a duffel bag.

"From top of the world to living on the street in just over a year. I lost everything, Morgan. Everything. I can't even think about my kids, them growing up without me as their dad, without wanting to scream or cry," he says with a hitch in his voice. "And then two more years on, this shit all happened, and the only reason I made it until then was I finally hit bottom hard enough to lose all of my pride and dignity and did whatever I could to make a few bucks along the way so I'd have somewhere to crash. Usually, it was a cruddy little motel that charged by the night, and some days, I'd sleep outside if the weather was good so I wouldn't have to skip too many meals. It sucked, but in a way, it was an honest life. I learned how to survive on the streets, to keep off the cops' radar whenever they swept us out, and so when the monsters came, I knew how to get off the grid better than normal people and hide. Once the first wave was over, I hit the bricks to get away from the city since there were so many of the zombies around, ended up at Marcus's place when I saw the signs, met him, and he decided I was useful so I could stay. I admit, it was nice to be needed and wanted again after all that time. I'm not proud now of being there but had no idea what was going on until it was too late. And here we are." He stops abruptly, but the story is done anyway.

Morgan had listened closely throughout, only nodding or adding an "mm-hmm" where needed, but inside, she boiled at what had happened to him. *It's a good thing I'm not going to meet Irene or Irene's boyfriend*, she thinks and then realizes karma has probably settled that score. But, being a fan of small people herself since they haven't developed the bad habits and crappy behavior of most adults just yet, she mourns for his kids. And for him. Impulse strikes her, not surprisingly. "Let's go see."

"Go see what?"

"See if your kids are still alive. Maybe not right now … or, yeah, maybe right now. My brother and everyone else will worry if we're late, but they'll be okay. Let's do it." She's already easing off the gas pedal without consciously thinking about it.

Bob is silent again, sitting pensively with his hands in his lap and head down. "I don't think so. I know they're gone, or am 99 percent sure they are, even though I'd like to think we'd drive there, pull up to the house, and they'd come running out, safe and sound. This may not make sense to you, but without seeing proof that they're gone, it feels like they're still here, in my memories just the same as they always were, smiling, happy, and all mine. If we somehow found them, and they were either dead or turned, I don't think I could handle it. It's better to remember them the way they were. Dammit, I miss them, and I hate that their faces aren't as clear in my mind as they used to be. I know that happens with memories, but I sure as hell don't like it."

Morgan finds that she has a lot to think about. Part of her is already planning yet another road trip at some point, but she also admires him, his love for his children and obvious love for his wife, even after what had happened. He was a survivor before most everyone else was a survivor; his grit is admirable. Parents sacrifice for their children and love them unconditionally, even when things don't go well. Maybe the whole parenting thing isn't as simple or one-sided as she thought. It makes her think back to her own childhood and her parents, who had tried so hard to rein her in, and recognizing, just maybe, they were trying to help her instead of control her, until she had pushed back so hard and so often that they gave up. She dances away from that thought before going too deep and, instead, reaches over and grabs Bob's hand and squeezes it, thinking maybe it isn't just to comfort *him*. It's quiet in the car for a good long while.

# CHAPTER 9

They drive out from under the cooling end-of-summer northern weather, finding the suffocating, dense humidity of the South lurking in wait as they leave Virginia and cross into North Carolina. Not that anyone knows what day or date it is any longer, but it's certainly the tail end of summer, though that season's heat lingers far longer in the South, as if reluctant to surrender its hold. This is the same mountain pass her brother came north on when he'd left home to seek the sanctuary of the lake, but she doesn't make the connection. Luckily for them, the crowd of zombies that had been puttering around the area dispersed after the death of the alpha that had been leading and coordinating them at the time, so there are no creatures stirring.

Bob has been sleeping restlessly for the last few hours since telling his tale, and Morgan's been relieved, in a way, for the silence; just focusing on the drive and little else, trying to dodge the thoughts he stirred up in her mind. Unlike the group's journey north, it's a clear evening, and the eastern vista is astonishing—she can see forever across the sprawling green fields, hills, and forests below them and feel the beach beckoning even though she knows it's well beyond her line of sight. It's nice to pretend sometimes.

Morgan is tempted to wake Bob so he can enjoy the view but decides against it. She's of the mind that if you're sleeping, you need the rest. She personally sleeps very little, even before the world became as dangerous as it is—it's difficult to settle the turmoil of her mind and anxious nature of her body, and she feels sleep is a patch of hours she could have otherwise been doing something, but has finally accepted everyone isn't the same. However, night is beginning its inexorable creep over the mountains above her, casting long shadows on the hills tapering down from the guardrails, and she realizes she's getting tired too. It has been a long day behind the wheel, especially at the high rate of speed which requires concentration beyond routine driving. They've been lucky to find mostly clear roads, which is the norm across the country. Apocalyptic movies in the past had always shown massive pileups all over the screen regardless of what kind of monster was invading, but the reality is people inside cars don't suddenly die from zombie attacks—people stupid enough to get *out* of their cars had been the ones who died, and as a result, the highways are largely deserted. But, big pileups make for good cinema. She thought it may be a little different near the huge population centers of major cities, where people would have tried to evacuate and maybe got stranded in the chaos, but Denver's roads had been pretty clear too. Anyway, they aren't going somewhere where they will have to worry about that since big populations of people end up being big populations of the undead, so it would be stupid to head to a large city.

The fatigue of being ready for surprises at an average between 80 and 100 miles an hour for close to 700 miles has taken a toll on her. She's only made a single stop along the way, not much after Bob told his story. They'd needed gas and a pee break, and now they need the same. Nighttime driving is a bad idea in any regard—too many chances of a zombie or two wandering into the road, or a clutch of deer or something else now that the animals have mostly reclaimed the earth and can meander as they please without fear of (normal) humans. Morgan's nothing if not physically self-aware and so lets the Corvette slow and ease onto one of the first exit ramps.

The change in engine tone brings Bob out of his slumber, and he mumbles a groggy, "Where are we?"

"Just across the NC state line, sleepyface." And he is—there's a big line running up his right cheek from the upholstery of the seat. She grins as she sees the added character line in the faint glow of the dashboard lights. "We're going to call it a night, and since you slept all day, you can have first watch."

"Okay, no problem. You should've woken me up sooner to keep you company. But, I admit I was tired, *really* tired after talking before. Thanks for letting me do that. Even though it's hard to think about them and everything that happened, I admit, I feel a little better letting some of it out of my head."

"You're welcome. Thanks for trusting me too. I'm sorry for everything you went through, and I'm glad you made it out the other side."

There's a forlorn convenience store with gas pumps standing guard over the parking lot just off the exit; it's dark inside like every other building, and the awning over the front doors scowls at them in the fading gloom of the day. They decide they can get food, water, and gas in the morning when they have better light.

After backing the grumbling car into a spot where they'll have a clear path of escape if needed, Morgan cracks the windows enough to allow air to circulate and hits the ignition button. The silence is a massive, echoing hollow to her ears at first after so many hours of the big V8 leading them south, but then the whir of cicadas rises and steadily surrounds them on all sides. At first, they step out of the car and simply listen for dragging footsteps within the cacophony of the bugs' racket, waiting for a few minutes with the doors closed but ready at hand.

Once satisfied that they're alone, they both do their business on opposite sides of the store and then return to the car but swap seats again so Bob can drive immediately if something happens. Jack takes a disinterested tour of the grounds, claims ownership of the right-hand corner of the store, and then hops back into the package space and curls up, ears rotating as he too stays on watch. Morgan's asleep almost before finishing the thought of how comfortable the car's seats are, even for sleeping. Bob sits virtually motionless in the driver's seat, alternating between watching the night fall heavily and peering at Morgan's slumbering form in the rising moonlight. She told him to wake her after a few hours, but he, too, is of a mind (thanks to parenthood) that if you're sleeping, you need it, and so he resolves to let her rest until she awakens on her own. Many months of living outdoors and being watchful at night—for police, for other homeless people looking to take advantage of their fellow unfortunates, for roving bands of kids who thought it was funny to roust and beat up the underbridge denizens—allow him complete focus and confidence he can stay up for as long as she stays down. It feels nice to keep an eye on someone too.

*** 

It's an uneventful night. Morgan sleeps all the way through until dawn bursts over the eastern horizon, promising a clear, hot day. While Bob rigs up the siphon pump her brother came up with for extracting gasoline from the underground tanks and begins fueling the Corvette, Morgan checks the doors to the store and finds them locked. One crisp strike through the glass with her Bo takes care of that, and she collects some bottled water to supplement what they already carry as well as some suspicious-looking nutrition bars and trail mix from the dusty shelves. Suspicious because she still struggles at times with the lack of freshly made food, loathing the list of unpronounceable preservatives and chemicals that make up the "nutrition" bars, but going hungry is a poor alternative.

They finish the morning necessaries and hit the road, now about 350 miles from the beach, so a much shorter day's driving lies ahead before they'll be there and able to scout out Hilton Head. A sprint down I-77 through Charlotte and on to Columbia before heading east on I-26 leading to good old 95 and the final hours, and they both munch breakfast happily at the prospect of completing the trip by early afternoon. The northern part of the state whizzes by, as does the Lake Norman area where her brother had been living when civilization crumpled and died with a feeble whimper, albeit with plenty of screaming in the beginning too. Once they're south of Charlotte, the roads are clearer than within the city limits, and Morgan lets the big motor pull them ever faster on the trip toward Columbia. They pass the dormant skeletons of the roller coasters scraping the sky at the theme park straddling the state line and carry on south, enjoying the sunny day with windows open despite the increasing temperature and humidity.

Like many parts of South Carolina, the roads are boring stretches of endless pines adjacent to the highway but little other scenery or small towns or cities to break up the view. You take the highway to get from here to there as quickly as you can, but sightseeing doesn't happen a whole lot. It's about an hour to Columbia where they'll pick up 26, and Morgan pushes the gleaming-red elegant brute of a car through the air, as if she's trying to teleport and skip the drive. That hour passes quickly, and she follows the long, sweeping ramp to join the eastern branch of 26's path. Her brother or Eve could have warned her, but Morgan isn't familiar with the roads here, of course, and eventually runs into a mistake. While 26 is well paved and fairly straight, there also is pretty much darn near nothing along the black asphalt ribbon heading toward the beaches. Very few towns or even rest stops adjacent to the route, and most locals know if you need gas, food, or a restroom break, you should either do so before leaving the Columbia area or be patient for the one semilarge exit along the way.

Which Morgan zooms past, even though the fuel gauge is nearing the ¼ mark, assuming there'll be another exit in a few miles. There is, but no services are marked on the signs, just another marker for Route 176 and nothing else, so she keeps going. What she finds instead about ten miles farther along is indeed a movie-worthy, catastrophic pileup. It's impossible to see what had happened to cause it, but dozens of vehicles are strewn across the entire road, mashed together, and spilling over to fill the gaps between the shoulders and the watchful, never-ending pine sentinels. She stops the car, leaving it running, and they step out to scan the wreckage.

She can see the undercarriages of cars lying on their sides, headlights facing back toward them, shrapnel from the collisions, clothes blown out of suitcases and scattered into the unkempt grass of the median. Twisted metal, glass, and rubber form an impenetrable barricade to the other side. A few bodies lie mingled with the cars, nothing moving, and they decide there isn't a need to get any closer. While years of violence and battles have hardened both of them against the presence, smell, and sad silence of the corpses that vastly outnumber the living, there's no need to actively inspect them. There's no question they're all dead and beyond help, so they stand their ground.

It looks like a giant child had been playing with the cars on the highway and then got bored and threw them together out of frustration or disinterest. There's no way they'll get the Corvette around it, and as they look across the median to the westbound lanes for alternatives, they see those, too, are completely blocked with debris. Frustrated, they get back inside the car. Morgan turns it around and heads back toward the west, looking for the last exit and now mindful of their dwindling gas situation.

"I think we'll be okay off that next exit. Most highways have a frontage road of sorts that runs parallel to it, so I bet that 176 will take us around all of that mess. I've seen several signs for that road along the way, so makes sense that it does since if it intersected the highway, we'd have only seen it once. Might have more to look at along the way, too, if it's a country road," Bob says as they near the exit and sweep onto the ramp.

There are indeed no gas stations in sight, just dusty pull-offs along the ramps in both directions. They find the road and turn to go east and carry on, seeing occasional flickers of light reflecting off metal and glass when the highway is closer to them. *Not a darn thing along this road either, country or not,* Morgan thinks, frustrated at the idea of being stranded somewhere soon and having to find a new set of wheels if they run out of fuel. She's also bothered by not being able to tell the trailing group about the big wreck here and how to get around it, but she has to trust they'll figure it out. It isn't like she can go make a big sign for them. While they've all agreed to stop and wait if they run into trouble, a detour doesn't count as the trouble they'd meant, so they're going to keep moving.

They pass the occasional driveway leading off like a runway into the trees, rutted paths of gravel and grass, but any houses are invisible from the road. She becomes ever more conscious of the gas gauge and is relieved when they come to an abandoned (of course) fruit and vegetable stand after a while, sitting along one of the brown pull-offs and in front of a sprawling space cut into the forest. *Surely, there'll be a gas can or two at a farm*, Morgan thinks, pulling over behind an old-fashioned wagon in the dirt parking lot. The wooden sign on the wagon's side promises "ORGANIC VEGGY'S & FRIUTS" in handwritten, fading-to-pink red paint, and there are some dried out somethings in shallow wooden trays on top of the wagon, clearly picked over by birds and other critters.

"Thank goodness we're stopping," Bob says with a yawn. "I'm out of my normal rhythm from staying up all night and was starting to get sleepy there. Where's a drive-thru Dunkin' Donuts when you need one?"

"Back at the exit twenty miles ago. Maybe they've got some fresh coffee here," Morgan answers sarcastically, annoyed by this interruption in their plans as she turns the car off, listening to the steady tick of the exhaust as it slowly cools and keeping her ears tuned for any other sounds. "It's probably 'organic' too. I bet they did in the old days, to scoop up some of the tourist dollars heading to the coast. We need gas, bad, so let's take a look around in that barn. Jack, go see," she says to the big shepherd and points toward the barn. He ignores her and happily goes over to nose his way around the wagon, looking for a treat of some kind, or perhaps a water bowl. "Good dog. Furry jerk," she says, bemused.

The barn is an ancient, listing structure that looks like it has been through too many temperamental thunderstorms and is waiting for one more to finish the job of knocking it over. The carriage door is ajar, leaving enough space for a human to fit through but not enough light to see what's inside. It stands fifty yards off the road, behind a small single-story house clad in what had once been a cheerful yellow siding but has seen better days too. Morgan's radar is on alert, and they return to the car before going any farther and arm themselves. Bob covers her with a shotgun while she creeps up to the opening of the barn, peeks in, and then tries to let her vision adapt to the darkness.

Nothing inside, or at least, nothing moving, and she sweeps through it quickly to emerge in the sunlight out back. No gasoline containers either, but she notices an aging sedan settling on partially flat tires parked behind the house, and she silently makes her way across the yard that had run riot, watching the windows of the house for motion. Jack trots over to join her, showing no sign of being bothered by anything, and she takes her cue from him and relaxes a little. Bob closes up behind as well. There's no one here, which isn't surprising, but it's always good to be careful.

They search all around the buildings and eventually find a small, empty, plastic gas container sitting on the seat of a lawn tractor tucked under the eave of the barn, and Bob manages to get a few gallons of gas out of the tanks of both the mower and the car, taking a few trips to transfer it all into their car. He says they'll have to keep their fingers crossed that there's no debris or water that'll gunk up the Corvette's sensitive engine, but they don't have a choice—it's take a chance or be ready to walk pretty soon. Now, they at least will have another eighty miles or so of range. Hopefully, there's enough to get the rest of the way to Hilton Head, but if not, maybe they'll at least get all the way out of this dead zone between somewhere and nowhere.

Morgan needs to go to the bathroom and is getting ready to ask Bob to head back to their car so she can do so in private behind the house, when she sees Jack's ears perk up. Immediately on full alert, she drops to her knees, whistles softly to Bob, and scans in every direction, looking for motion in the tree line. She feels like they're terribly exposed out in the open space and wonders if the house is unlocked so they'll have shelter if needed.

Then she hears it. The hum of an engine cutting through the silence. Not an exotic one, in fact, it sounds like one of the cylinders is occasionally misfiring as the sound increases, coming from the way they'd been driving. She waves Bob over to her and reaches down to steady the dog, and the three of them peer around the corner of the house.

After a few minutes of the engine noise increasing, they watch a well-worn brown pickup truck drive past the roadside stand, trailing a light cloud of dust. Initially, they hold still as it continues down the road, but then they look at each other in mild surprise—they haven't found anyone "new" in a long time, and at first, they're stunned into inaction. Then, Morgan realizes they need to get moving and sprints over to the car and climbs in quickly, not wanting to lose sight of the truck.

"Come on, hurry!" she shouts through the window as she fires the 'Vette back up. Bob and Jack reach the car and pile in, and she sweeps out of the parking area in a spray of dirt and gravel and then with a chirp of the wide tires as they reach the asphalt and fight for traction.

As she accelerates through the gears, closing the gap between the receding truck and their car, Morgan starts to think back over the past thirty minutes. They stopped for at least fifteen minutes, and so any dust they'd stirred would've settled back to the ground by now. And, they'd parked behind the wooden wagon so the car would've been largely hidden to any passersby. With the three of them being around the back of the house as the truck had gone by, it all pointed to them likely being unnoticed by the driver of the pickup. Whoever it is wouldn't have seen them beforehand coming off the highway, waited a bit, and then followed, only to leapfrog them by accident, right? She shakes off her misgivings, encouraged by the thought of meeting someone (or more), maybe getting additional fresh gas so they can complete the trip, some real food, and that now overdue bathroom break she has just skipped, but subconsciously, she reduces her speed—no longer closing the distance but maintaining it.

"What are you doing?" Bob asks.

"Nothing. Just following them, or him, or whoever it might be. No need to jump into their rearview. Might be better to follow on our terms and see where they go. Maybe we can get more gas, and some food, and stuff. Find out if they've been over to the beach and can tell us anything helpful."

"True. Wonder if they have a couch I can crash on. I'm just dragging."

"Well, don't fall asleep now, Pops. You can take a little 'old man' nap later on."

"Jesus, Morgan. I'm in my late forties, not eighties, for crying out loud. Shit, you know what? I might be fifty now. Hard to tell without a calendar anymore."

"Happy birthday. We can stop and find you a black cake and candles later, and maybe some 'old man' underpants, stool softener, and hearing aids too, Gramps."

"Remind me to wipe some of my 'old man' boogers or ear wax on your face next time you fall asleep. Just wait until you get older. I'm going to make fun of your saggy tits and droopy ass once gravity catches up."

"That's never, *ever* going to happen. You're going to be able to bounce a quarter off my firm ass until I'm seventy. Well, *you're* not going to because you won't be lucky enough to get near my ass, and by the time I'm seventy, we'll have buried you a *long* time beforehand."

"I guess it could be worse. Most guys my age are dead already. Hell, most guys of all ages are dead, period. Me, I'm driving to the beach in a red Corvette with a much-younger hot chick. An obnoxious one but still."

She punches him in the shoulder and laughs. They're excited to meet someone new, and they keep up the playful banter as they follow the truck's wake, unable to see it, but tracking the faint dusty trail it leaves behind.

\*\*\*

After a few miles, they come over a gentle rise that had hidden the road ahead of them and notice the dust is gone. Looking left and right since pickup trucks rarely disappear, Bob sees a driveway leading off into the trees on his side just a few dozen yards back, a faint whirligig of disturbed air floating at its head. Morgan reverses and turns in. Her senses are alert, but that's nothing new—the updated world makes you watch everything all the time.

Like all the other driveways they've seen, this one appears to just go into the woods indefinitely, so Morgan putters along carefully, mindful of the Corvette's low chassis. The cloud of dust is back, which is good, and another mile or so brings them around a bend in the road and a few hundred yards short of a small brick home tucked under ancient, looming trees shading the roof and front porch, which is adorned with a pair of black rocking chairs and some assorted other mismatched stools and benches. A birdbath sits askew on the front lawn, such as it is, and the rest of the lawn is cluttered here and there with typical country debris—a pile of tires, a rusting wheelbarrow, a lawn mower that has grass growing up between its wheels, and so on. Morgan pauses, just looking. The truck is parked out front, though no one is visible, and she slides the car back into first gear to go the rest of the way.

"Hold up a second," Bob says quickly.

"What? Seems okay, or do you see something? Not that your eyesight can be all that good now that you're in your second half century and all."

"That's just it. I don't see anything. That kind of bothers me. No dust in front of us. We've been following it for miles, like that character from Charlie Brown. I forget his name but remember he always, *always* had it around him. So where did this guy's go?"

"Hmmm. Good point."

They stay in the car but look around again and back over their shoulders. Finally, Morgan spots another dwindling swirl of dust to their rear, mostly hidden between a clutch of cypress trees that leads off into the woods from the driveway. "There's some kind of path off to the side it looks like. He or she maybe pulled off and around. But why?"

"I bet they've seen us following them. But if they did, and they were nervous, why go down a dead-end road? Something's funny, but not funny ha-ha. What are we missing?"

They turn off the car and get out, followed by Jack. He stays at Morgan's heel, and she's glad for that since he's their early-warning system. The pressure in her bladder is insistent now, and she really wants to get it over with but not until they figure out whatever's going on here. Both of them scan the house for signs of the driver, but the distance and deep shadows cast by the trees make seeing into the small windows impossible. Why won't the person come out to see them? Fear? Maybe—the remaining survivors have stayed alive by being careful for the last few years. They move slowly along the rutted driveway, on the shoulders, looking up and down, left and right, taking a step, checking again.

Bob finally sees it. A thin filament of fishing wire strung across the driveway at ankle height and trailing off between two scruffy saplings into denser undergrowth. He kneels down to see better and follows the line, without touching it, to the ends. A drab-green rectangular box is at the end of the string on either end. "I know what these are. Claymore mines. They've been used by the military for a long time. Really common in Vietnam. You point them toward your enemy, set the trip wire, and when it's triggered, they explode and blow a shit-ton of shrapnel in a shaped expanding cone toward the target area. Nasty things, these. If we'd rolled farther forward, they'd have both gone off, and we'd be dead meat in the driveway, even through the car," he says as he stands up from inspecting them and moves back out from the undergrowth. "So now what? They drove to the side, either because they saw us and wanted us to trip the wire and die, or because they always have to since the mines are there. Those would sure handle any roaming squads of zombies and give them plenty of heads up that they were being invaded."

Morgan chews her lower lip thoughtfully, wondering if they should just go back the way they came and leave this place alone. Not that she isn't up for a fight most times, but since joining this tiny group of survivors, she's slowly come to the realization that others rely on her, and rushing headlong into something that could get her injured or killed has broader implications than it did in the past.

Just as she's deciding to do just that—back up and beat it—the front door of the house opens, and a man steps onto the porch. "Hey there! Don't come any closer on the driveway. There are mines in the bushes. Let me come out to you," he calls and then steps down onto the yard. "Say, that's a nice car."

*Why does everyone say that?* Morgan thinks, figuratively throwing her hands up.

She eyes him as he gets closer, wondering if he's been watching all along, has seen them find the string and mines, or has been busy in the house and is only now just noticing them. Home defense makes a lot of sense—they did the same up at the lake. This is the middle of freaking nowhere, but the zombies have had plenty of time to wander anywhere over these past years.

Speaking sotto voce to Bob, she asks, "Stay or go?"

"I think we're okay, don't you?"

She isn't sure, but her self-confidence earned by decades of jumping off a perfectly good whatever into the unknown and figuring it all out while in midair makes the decision easy. That and the fact that she feels like she's going to burst if she doesn't pee soon. "I think so. Let's be careful though.

Wait, Jack," she says as she grabs for him. He had started to move toward the man now closing in on them, and the wire is still between them all.

The approaching man is an unassuming one. Perhaps early forties, dark hair peppered with strands of white at the temples and over his ears, and the beginning stages of good old male-pattern baldness winning the fight on his forehead. He's fairly short, not more than five and a half feet tall, and slender. Short compared to Morgan at least. Unlike most of the people they've run into over time, he isn't in good physical shape. Skinny, yes, but not carrying any of the either new or lifelong muscle that's typical of the survivors. Clean-shaven with charcoal eyes peering out from under dense eyebrows meeting in the middle above his nose like a misplaced moustache, he keeps walking toward them and then stops well short of the trip wire. He's wearing hiking boots, new ones, and a clean pair of black jeans with a black Falcons T-shirt untucked at the waist. Again, not like everyone else—he looks as though nothing has happened. Clean clothes, no stubble of a beard, and none of the visible wear and tear of the stress of a dying species being hunted by their own morbid and murderous creation.

One of Morgan's weak spots, outside of her wildly competitive nature or maybe because of it, is that if she's faced with someone she deems physically inferior and, therefore, unthreatening to her in that way, she tends to disregard them. Most of the time, that works out fine for her since she's fast, strong, and more aggressive than your typical person, and so if she's wrong, she's able to make her way out of trouble on the fly. This is what happens now—this man can't "take" her, and she feels her guard dropping; the suspicions that have been tickling her subconscious relax into the background.

"Hi. Um, I guess welcome to my place?" he says with a slight upward lilt at the end of the sentence, turning a statement into a semiquestion. "You need to watch that wire. I've got it set pretty heavy so a squirrel won't set it off or anything, but it's still pretty twitchy. Can't let visitors just stroll in here unannounced. The monsters, whatever they are, can be kinda quiet sometimes. Who are you? How did you find me?"

"I'm Morgan, and this is Bob. Thanks for warning us about the wire. We saw your truck out on the road and followed you. We were stopped when you went by, so we were kind of chasing your dust trail." Whether he knows they had seen the wire before he came outside or not, there's no reason to show all their cards to a stranger.

"What are y'all doing? Where are you from? Where are you headed?"

"We came from up in New York, and we were going to Hil … the beach," she answers, annoyed at herself for the hitch.

"Oh, Hilton Head, yeah, nice place but full of noisy Yankees most of the warm months. Not them baseball ones, but you know, folks from up that way. I guess like y'all now that I think about it. No offense intended. I'm Charles. Well, 'Chad' to my friends. Nice to meet you."

"None taken. Nice to meet you too. I'm guessing there are a lot less noisy everyones out there nowadays. Have you been?"

"Oh, ayuh. You're right, not much out there now 'cept seagulls and deer. Lots quieter now. It's nice, though I don't get over that way much, don't need to. Mostly have what I need here, and going out can be dangerous, if you know what I mean."

Bob is glad to hear it's quiet on the island since it's a large one, and if they have to really thoroughly sweep it clear, it could literally take them years. He, too, is put at ease by Chad's mild country mannerisms and smaller stature.

"Well, why don't y'all come in for a drink and set for a spell? The beach'll be there anyway. I've got some gas, food, and water, too, if you could use some of that. Mind your step and go around that tree there," he says, pointing to a mammoth evergreen to the left of the driveway and outside the end of the fishing line. "That way, you won't stomp on a stick that flips up and yanks the wire and *kaboom* by accident," he adds, miming an explosion with his hands as he does so. "If you don't mind, can the dog stay outside? I've got allergies to them."

Bob and Morgan glance at each other, questions in their eyes, and then shrug. He's right that the beach will be there, and they're mindful of their fuel supply. It's one thing to know they can get there, maybe, but if they have to get lost in a hurry, it won't do to be near empty. Running from zombies sucks, especially with Bob's maimed Achilles. Morgan leads Jack around the tree, asks if there's anything else to worry about, and when Chad says there isn't, lets the big dog loose to do his thing. Now that they're all introduced and defused, Morgan's need to pee returns to the point where she's cramping. Or is she *cramping*, cramping? She isn't sure. She doesn't keep close track of her cycle anymore, but she needs the bathroom either way, and damn soon.

They enter the house, Jack remaining outside to do whatever it is dogs do in a new place—mostly sniff, piss, repeat until really just pretend peeing—and walk through a short entryway and into the kitchen which is decorated in classic country with brown cabinets, a blue-and-white tablecloth on the table where settings have already been laid out for two; matching curtains block the view to the backyard. A short hallway leads off to the left and seems to be toward a bedroom. A narrow hall is on the right as well with a series of varnished wooden doors, all closed, down its length. It's as neat as a pin inside. No dust, no clutter, no pile of stuff in the sink or on the counters. They were the same way at the lake—since time is now "free" compared to the past, everyone seems to be better about picking up after themselves. It even smells clean, like bleach and furniture polish.

Morgan notices a faint hum, looks around for the source, and realizes it's coming from the outdated refrigerator tucked into its niche in the bland taupe laminate counters. It takes a second for it to register. "You have power?"

"Yes'm. Sure do. I've got a real quiet generator out back inside a shed to keep it even quieter. Took some trying out different kinds before I got one that was quiet enough so that those fuckin' critters didn't come 'round. Went through a buncha mines there for a bit. Pardon my language there. How about that drink?"

Bob answers, "Yes, please, if it's no trouble."

"No trouble at all. Here you go," Chad says as he fishes a pitcher out of the fridge and pours it into two smooth, clear glasses. Bob drinks half of his off in a single draft with a happy "Ahhh."

"You're not having any?" Morgan asks. She's been put at ease by his comfortable manner—and manners, for that matter—but skepticism runs deep in her nature, both before and after the world had gone through its massive hiccup of late.

"No'm. I drank a good bit of coffee before running out on errands, and I've found if I drink much water after that in the morning, I pee just about every five minutes."

"Oh, speaking of that, does your toilet work too?"

"Why wouldn't it? You just do your thing into the bowl, not like that can be broken. Oh. You mean can it flush after. Yep, sure does just fine. Septic out here. Cain't get on the county water this far out, but that finally turned out to be a good thing, I suppose." He waves a hand down the narrow hallway. "Third door on your right is the commode."

Morgan is reminded of her bathroom trip back in Kansas, when she first went through Marcus's compound. Marcus had given her the immediate creeps, as did the body language and overall feel of the people there—something just not right, and, of course, she'd been right but hadn't imagined the level of depravity there until Kuniko told her quickly outside the port-a-johns. Her consciousness is now telling her everything is fine here, that Chad's simply a survivor out in the middle of nowhere in a low-population area even in the past, and there's nothing to be worried about. But, she muses as she goes down the hall, the fact that she's having this conversation inside her head means some part of her disagrees.

The bathroom is immaculate, too, with the same gingham curtains from the kitchen carried on here. They make it dim and private, and out of what's now a habit, Morgan doesn't bother flicking the light switch. The seat and lid are down as she enters, and she hurries to lower her shorts and panties and sit before soiling herself or the vinyl floor. Relief! It's been a long time since she's sat on a normal toilet or had to go this badly. *Small pleasures these days*, she thinks. It feels like an evening when she had a rare handful of beers and gone for the first time—an endless stream courses out of her, and she looks around the small room while she relishes the easing of the sharp pressure in her belly.

Nothing catches her eye until she needs to wipe. The toilet paper holder is empty—typical man. A little annoyed, she stand squats with her britches hindering her ankles and looks inside the vanity. Luckily, there's a spare roll there, and she'd have overlooked the tiny gold ring underneath the roll if one of its stones hadn't caught on the toilet paper and fallen off with a tiny *pat* onto the vinyl. Taking care of the paperwork at the same time, she picks up the ring and studies it in the shadowy light. A female's ring, no doubt about that since it's too small and delicate for a man. So a woman has been, or is, here. A small woman, or someone younger, since the ring doesn't fit any of Morgan's fingers, even her pinkie. She doesn't like that thought at all and finishes her business, flushes—wonders for a second at fully functioning plumbing—and tidies up, slipping the ring into the front pocket of her shorts as she does so. Morgan intends to go back out there, collect Bob, and politely get the fuck out. Something's wrong here, and while part of her wants to confront Chad and maybe pick a fight, something else—responsibility to the group perhaps—is winning the argument and says to just go.

That argument is totally settled, however, when she returns to the kitchen. Bob's head is down on his arms on the kitchen table, and he's snoring lightly. She's only been gone for a couple of minutes, and he's out cold? He's been saying he's tired, and he's old, maybe even fifty, but still.

"Have a seat and a drink of water," Chad says.

"No, but thank you. I feel much better now, but I think we need to get back on the road. I appreciate your hospitality though." She nudges Bob's arm. "Hey, lazybones old man, wake up. It's time to go."

Nothing. Just another snore and vague mumble. She pushes him again with the same result.

Chad's tone is a little firmer this time. "Seems like your friend is taking a nap. Maybe you need to sit down and rest yourself."

Morgan doesn't much like the look in Chad's eyes now. Trying to keep her breathing steady so as not to alert him, Morgan takes a deep breath through her nose, feeling the flood of adrenaline kick up and prepping her to do some serious damage to Chad.

"No, no, I don't think so," he says, while swinging a pistol around from behind his back to point it steadily at her torso. "I see what you're doing there, all those muscles bunching up and gettin' ready to move. Sit down, right now."

Shit.

"We're just going to have us a little chat with Chad now. Bob there is gonna sleep for a couple of hours prob'ly, so no point in pestering him. You and me are going to have us a little palaver, and depending on how that all goes, we'll see what happens after. Though you look like a keeper, I have to say."

He leers openly at her now, casting his greedy gray eyes up and down her figure, pausing at all the typical spots men linger on when it comes to a woman's body. She's dressed for comfort, wearing a simple dark-blue sports bra and running shorts, so there isn't much imagination needed.

Morgan's furious and thinking furiously. The dog's outside so will be of no help, plus all her weapons are still in the car. Chad's greeting had fooled them into laziness and stupidity. He must have drugged Bob with something, and Bob is too big for her to carry. Well, maybe she can carry him, but it sure wouldn't be far or fast. She feels trapped, and angry, but stuck.

"Sit the *fuck* down, woman!" Chad screams at her, slamming his free hand on the table, which makes her start. Bob doesn't even budge, but Morgan hears Jack bark from outside at the sudden noise. Good, he isn't wandering the woods, so he may be useful after all.

She reluctantly sits, never taking her eyes off the barrel of the pistol and noticing unhappily that his hand is unwavering. Sitting means her first move, if there'll be one, is going to be slower. But, if he meant to kill them, they'd be dead already, so that gives her some chance. The ideas he may have in mind are pretty obvious—he's a man out in the woods without company for a couple of years, so maybe her looks will allow her to distract him enough for an escape. She ponders how to try that and absent-mindedly reaches for the glass on the table in front of her, forgetting it's probably drugged and not seeing the widening grin on Chad's face as she does so.

What Morgan does see, however, is the reflection of movement behind her in the smooth surface of the water glass. If it had been empty, there would have been no chance. There's nothing she can make out clearly, but it's enough to spark her into motion. That glimpse and her outrageous reflexes are the only things that keep the rifle butt aimed at the back of her head from connecting. She lunges forward first with all the urgency of anger, flipping the table up and toward Chad, and tosses the glass at him in the same moment, trying to create as much visual clutter as she can. Bob's slumbering form falls off the table and hits the floor with a bony *thud*. Morgan dives off the chair to her left and tumbles across the floor and onto her feet before the rifle stops moving. Instead of pausing to assess what's going on, she does what she always does—moves like a cat on speed and launches herself at Chad, slamming her right arm on his gun hand. The pistol fires, deafening in the small kitchen, but the bullet whacks harmlessly off the floor. Well, harmlessly to Morgan anyway since it ricochets.

"You fucking shot me, Chad!" shouts the woman across the kitchen from her.

"I'm sorry, Daisy! I didn't mean it. Get her!"

"She's a pretty one, so don't hurt her. I want to keep her to play with!"

Morgan stares for a moment, and it's almost a moment too long when she needs to be moving. The woman is huge, not in girth, but taller than Morgan and bulkier, with dense muscles rippling down tattooed arms decorated with fantasy-themed ink running from both wrists and disappearing upward underneath a black skintight tank top. No original skin remains uncolored on her arms. One of those tattoos is now spoiled by a superficial red furrow from the bullet, which has skinned a skull's eye off her right bicep. Her black hair is cropped closely to her skull, and she has piercings through her eyebrows and nose and scattered up and down both ears. Where Chad has a wide-open, trustworthy face—at least, before he turned into a homicidal asshole—the woman's is severe and cruel.

Years ago, Morgan had flown to Paris with a boyfriend. She isn't a fan of flying, not due to fear, but because she likes to see everything along the way on a trip. Looking out over clouds and nothingness for hours agitates her since she feels like she's missing something. Her endlessly restless nature also prevents her from sleeping on planes and skipping the tedium, so to fight the boredom of the red-eye flight, she grabbed a handful of books at random from one of the kiosks in the international terminal. One of those was about an ex-army guy who had wandered the country, getting into various scraps and righting a lot of wrongs along his way. His name was Teacher, or Preacher, or something like that; it isn't coming to her in the heat of the moment, but what does is his philosophy of fighting as dirty and hard as you can. There's no fighting politely, especially not when outnumbered, and his mantra had been to hit first, hit hard, and put your opponent down as fast and permanently as possible. The concept makes wonderful sense to her since she lives in a state of near ignition at all times, and in these new no-holds-barred days, Morgan can exercise that to its fullest. Which is what she does now.

She's still close to Chad after having hit his arm, and as he fights for his grip on the pistol, she spins fully around, gaining momentum as she twists her torso into the blow and utterly pulps his nose with her elbow. Blood splashes across his face in a crimson smear, and he drops to the floor with a cry, clutching the shattered center of his face and losing the gun. Morgan delivers a heavy kick to his balls to further slow him, and one of his hands shoots down to cradle his damaged nuts. He's out of it for a minute at least. Daisy is hurriedly reversing the rifle she'd tried to hit Morgan with, and Morgan dives across the floor in another tumble, scooping one of the spilled knives from the table settings off the floor. A wild shot from the gun goes over her head, smashing bird shot against the cabinets in a mad clatter.

"You hurt Chad! I'm goin' to get you for that, bitch. Stop moving!" the woman cries.

*There are two place settings! I should have seen it earlier,* Morgan thinks wildly as she comes to her feet, ducks under the woman's awkward left hook, and then with all the malice she can muster, drives the butter knife through the soft skin under her opponent's chin and up through the roof of her mouth.

If Chad's injury was messy, Daisy's is a volcano of blood, spraying in a grisly gusher all over her shirt and tattoos. The woman lurches back from the strike, dropping the rifle and falling backward to the floor, gurgling sounds and frothy blood erupting from her ruined mouth. One, two stutters of her legs, and then she's still. Chad is silent on the other side of the room, curled up in a ball. He's either playing possum or out cold. She doesn't know, but she'll find out in a moment.

Morgan stands above Daisy for a second, still flaming with rage and looking for an outlet. She's magnificent in triumph, if someone had been conscious to see her. Muscles bunched and rippled from her shoulders to her wrists, the gleam of sweat across her chest, hair unbound and askew in a dark halo around her stunning face. She's fully, wildly alive. The fight is over so quickly that she feels like the blood has just begun pumping into her muscles, and she almost wishes for more of them or a half-dozen zombies to battle.

As she works to still her breathing, she hears Jack barking madly outside and thinks she's gotten her wish. Almost happily, she scoops the pistol and shotgun off the floor and

races to the front door, hopping lightly over Daisy's prone form. Once she opens the door, she sees nothing; Jack simply heard the commotion and is trying to get in to help. "Good dog. C'mon."

They go back in, where Jack sniffs his way through the mess in the kitchen and then pisses on Daisy's upturned face before exploring the rest of the house. Morgan checks on Bob, who's still asleep on the floor but breathing steadily. She drags him unceremoniously by his feet out into the den to avoid the steadily spreading puddles of blood, hoists him onto the couch with some effort, and then walks back into the kitchen to see about Chad. The ring from the bathroom and the pair of them trying to capture her, or worse, bothers her, and she wants some answers, though she has at least a hint of what has happened here in mind.

No point in being nice now either, so she leans down over Chad's prone form and raps him on the forehead with the butt of his own pistol. Not gently. "Wake up, asshole. We are indeed going to have ourselves a little … what did you say before? *Palaver*. You're not going to enjoy it."

He doesn't move, but she figures from his injuries, he's faking it. A mashed nose and nuts are probably really uncomfortable but not consciousness threatening, so she stands up and aims the gun at his knee.

"You have until I count back from three before I put a bullet through your left knee. Three, two, one."

*Bang!*

Chad screams as he lurches up in an odd sit-up move to grab his knee, or rather what's left of it. Heavy-caliber bullets from two feet away do incredible damage. "You shot me, you bitch!"

"Did you think I was kidding, Chad? I warned you. Seems only fair. You shot Daisy, she tried to shoot me, I shot you."

Morgan's surprisingly calm now, almost clinical. Maybe it's because she knows she needs to be removed emotionally from the moment. She fully intends to torture him if needed to get answers, and she wants to focus on that versus the pain she's prepared to inflict to one of the few remaining humans.

Squatting down, Morgan waves the pistol around as she speaks. In another context, a gorgeous woman wearing snug and flattering clothes would have been alluring, but the casual menace of the gun's movements and the detached way she speaks makes it anything but a sensual moment. "We're going to play a game, you piece of shit. I ask a question, you answer *promptly*, or I shoot something else. I don't know how long you'll be able to play, but I seem to have enough bullets to continue for a bit if you decide not to answer at any point. And I think we've erased any doubt about whether I'll pull the trigger."

He groans from the floor, unsure which maimed body part to hold. Blood flows from his mashed nose and from the ruin that used to be his knee. He catches sight of Daisy's prone form and moans. "You killed Daisy? Why would you do that?"

"That's a dumb question, Chad. You don't get to ask questions anyway." She feels a strange, comforting certainty come over her and realizes she doesn't plan on letting him live either, no matter what he says, but doesn't feel like that's something to share just yet. "Why do you have this ring?" she asks as she digs it out of her pocket and drops it on his chest.

He only stares up at her, maybe finally truly understanding how this is going to turn out. He previously hasn't taken his eyes from the looming barrel of the pistol, watching the tunnel of pain meander around the room, now toward his face, now his torso, now his legs. Above the bloody mess of his nose, those gray eyes glare back, but he presses his lips together and gives a small shake of his head.

Sigh. *Okay then. The hard way.*

*Bang!*

More screaming as his hands jump to the new injury to his other leg. Morgan has fired through the meaty part of his upper thigh, not too far from his crotch. More blood, lots of it. She isn't aware of it, but she's grimly smiling. Not because she enjoys doing this to him, but because she instinctively seeks to balance the scales when people mistreat women. She's sure Chad and Daisy have something like that going on here, maybe even back to before, and she's determined to find out what it is and even the score.

"Chad, I don't think you're taking me seriously. I'll remind you of the rules. I ask, you answer, or ka-pow goes the gun. Are we clear on that?"

He only moans and barely makes eye contact this time, surely in agony with two close-range gunshot wounds added to the earlier injuries. She lets him roll around for a minute, thinking maybe he'll come around to telling the truth.

Once his breathing slows, a little, she asks again. "Ready for another countdown? Remember, it starts with three and ends with one and then pew-pew, but a lot louder and more painful if I don't get anything from you. Three, two …"

"Fuck you," he sneers weakly through the sheet of blood coursing down his face. "I'm not telling you anything. You're not going to kill me."

"You know what? I believe you that you're not going to talk, and you're right. I'm not going to kill you. People don't usually kill people. Guns held by people kill people. And much faster."

*Bang!*

\*\*\*

It's a mess in the kitchen with nothing new to see, so Morgan leaves that room alone. While Bob is still sleeping off whatever cocktail they gave him, she figures she should look around and see about finding some answers to her question. There are two bedrooms down the same hall as the bathroom. One is neatly made up, which makes her think it's Chad's room. The other is a tumble back into adolescence—rock 'n' roll posters hanging all over the walls, a lava lamp cycling purple goop on the corner of a bookcase filled with sword-and-sorcery-type fantasy books that must have been the inspiration behind Daisy's tattoo collection, dark clothes littering the floor in unkempt piles, and a pornographic movie running on a small television hung from a ceiling bracket. Morgan only glances at the screen, noticing it's "normal" sex being performed, before savagely ripping the TV off its mount to shatter on the floor.

She swings back out to the room where Bob is snoozing and checks there too—lots of movies in the credenza which holds a larger television, a mix of action-adventure, some zombie titles, and a handful of more adult films. Not really anything out of the ordinary, though she wonders about the relationship between Chad and Daisy. Siblings? Lovers? Something weirder than that?

*No way to find out now,* her own inside voice reminds her.

Still no clues about the little ring. Maybe it's from when Daisy was younger, just forgotten under the sink for years and years? Probably not, but there's nothing else in the house indicating there are or have been other people here.

Tiring of the stench of blood mixed with gunpowder hovering in a poisonous cloud, and frustrated at being unable to find anything, Morgan drifts outside and stands on the porch, surveying the property. She sits down on a black rocking chair, scanning and thinking and allowing the remaining adrenaline of the fight work its way out of her system. Still unsatisfied by the abbreviated fight and lack of answers, she almost reluctantly lets the peace and quiet of the wooded clearing relax her. The spare sheen of sweat she worked up dries quickly as she rocks.

There's nothing she hasn't already seen out front, so once she fully calms down, she stands back up and walks around to the back of the house and sees a compact single-story yellow building that's constructed to look like a miniature barn, trimmed in a happy red with a green standing seam metal roof. It looks new, or at least newly painted. There's a single side-to-side rolling door out front, which is closed. She isn't going to be unarmed this time, but she checks the ammo in both the pistol and shotgun just in case. Five rounds for the handgun and three for the bigger gun—that should be enough for anything. She creeps toward the barn, aware she can't see through the one window to the left of the door thanks to the glare from the sun, so her nerves are on a hair trigger.

With the pistol tucked into her waistband and the shotgun at the ready, she almost kills Bob. He'd coughed wetly behind her, so she spun and fired before thinking. At the last microsecond, she realized it could be him and lifted the barrel of the gun into the air, sending the bird shot pellets harmlessly into the blue sky.

"Jesus, Morgan. What the hell? You about shot me. What are you doing, and what on earth happened inside the house? You made a hell of a mess, and who is the scary tattooed and pierced woman with the extra piercing in her tongue? That's nasty." He looks groggy and tired as he walks toward her unsteadily. She steers him back to the porch, with an uneasy glance behind her at the barn, and fills him in on everything that had gone down—the ring, the fight, maybe glossing over the details of what she did to Chad a little bit. "Holy crap. I'm sorry I was out of it. I never thought to suspect anything, and the water smelled and tasted fine. No idea what might have been in it to knock me out cold so fast."

"If I hadn't had to pee so badly, I would've been in the same boat, so don't feel bad. He seemed to be harmless and welcoming. We needed gas and a break, and seeing another person made us let our guard down. That's never going to happen again, that's for sure. God knows what would be going on right now if I'd drunk it too." She shivers, angry and upset still, and then asks him if he feels up to covering her while she checks out the barn.

"Sure, but what are you hoping to find?"

"To be honest with you, I'm kind of hoping to find nothing at all. I'm so tired of it—people treating others badly, the abuse, the negativity, selfishness. Even now, when there are almost none of us left. I just … I just want to go to the beach and be happy."

"I know what you mean. We could just go and not look."

"You know I can't."

He just nods toward the barn. "Yeah, I do. Let's finish it then."

***

Bob holds the shotgun as Morgan creeps to the edge of the barn's door. She listens for a few moments, trying to find anything in the murky South Carolina humidity and stillness that sounds awry. Nothing. She slides the door open suddenly and darts back to the side, aware that Bob is now in the line of fire while she's safe. Again, nothing. Not rushing, she looks directly into the gloom of the open center section of the building to allow her eyes to adjust to the dark instead of rushing in and being effectively blind for a minute. Still nothing, other than the silhouette of a truck.

Motioning to Bob to hold his position and to keep the dog with him, Morgan enters, still on high alert and aware of any sounds or movement in the shadows. It's silent, and there are no smells other than the musty odor of dust and dirt. Like most barns, even though this is a compact one, there are stalls on either side of the middle section, though these are full-sized doors instead of those for horses. Each is padlocked. Two per side, about the size of a large coat closet, and there's another rolling door at the back. She slides past the black pickup and opens the rear door to allow more light inside.

Now, she waves Bob in. There isn't any danger here that's going to jump out at them, so they're just going to do some investigation of those locked doors. Jack trots along behind him.

"Anything?" Bob asks.

"No people anyway. I'm going to pop these locks off and see what's behind the doors. Say, that's a nice truck." It's a lifted ebony Toyota Tacoma, with "4x4" stickers on the rear fenders, a lightbar atop a roll bar in the bed that looks as powerful as a floodlight to summon Batman, oversized knobby tires for off-roading, and four doors. Not as big as the truck they've been using in New York, but it will fit four people and maybe five in a pinch. She glances inside and sees a key fob sitting on the driver's seat.

*Now, that's not smart. Someone could just steal it. Well, there aren't many someones around anymore, and we are in the middle of goddamn nowhere. Now that I think of it, though, I might be the one stealing it, if it even counts as stealing when the owner is dead.*

At first, she's going to shoot the locks off the doors, having seen that often enough in movies, but then the idea of holding the pistol close enough to the arch of the bolt in order to hit it seems risky. What about shrapnel? Or ricochets? Injuries are far more serious these days without hospitals and doctors, so Morgan looks around for a safer way to get it open. She sees a barrel off in a corner with a handful of rakes, shovels, and finally, a five-foot-long crowbar. She hefts it out and wedges it into the first lock and is about to heave down when Bob interrupts her.

"Hey, I've got that," he says, walking to her and handing her the shotgun.

Morgan smirks—inside her head, out of politeness—and pauses, but then takes his gun and steps to the side. She is, after all, the most capable person she knows, and so his good-natured attempt at chivalry irks and amuses her at the same time. But she can't fault him for being decent, so she'll let him go first and hands him the bar.

Bob is in okay shape for a guy his age, but that's more a function of their fight for survival over the past couple of years. Morgan's fitness is due to decades of pushing her limits, both physical and mental, and she has no doubt that despite his weight advantage, she's stronger than he is. She's right—it doesn't go well.

He strains to steadily lower the crowbar but gets nowhere, and after a few unproductive minutes, he gives up, red faced and sweaty. "No way we're going to get that open. That sucker is on there tight."

Smiling (again, inside), Morgan takes the bar from him and re-wedges it into the small opening between the body and shackle. Before giving a try, she resists the thought of failing once to make him feel better and also holds in the temptation of a biting comment about his attempt. She's a little proud of herself for that, especially as she realizes he's likely a bit embarrassed. He's the guy after all and, as he's told her, has spent his life doing and providing for others, but he has come up short. Both now and, according to his former wife, before too.

Thanks to her extensive martial arts training and other sports, Morgan knows how to coordinate every muscle in her body for maximum effort and impact, and she preps for the sharp downward leverage she's going to apply. When she does burst into motion, it's a smooth top-to-bottom action, applying every ounce of weight she has and all her strength but making it look effortless. The lock snaps into pieces like an egg dropped on the floor. Bob gapes at her, astonished she'd made it look so easy.

"Just lucky. You must have loosened it," she says casually, dropping the bar and opening the door to look inside.

Guns. Lots of guns. And more mines, like the ones protecting the driveway—several wooden crates of those. Rifles, pistols, boxes of assorted ammunition, hand grenades. A treasure trove of killing tools. Whatever Chad and Daisy had been up to here, they certainly accumulated enough weapons to fight off any number of zombies that showed up and then some.

"Holy shit!" Bob exclaims as he looks over her shoulder. "We're going to need to take all of that with us. Think about it. There are two bridges onto Hilton Head, and that's it for getting on or off the island. I can rig up all these claymores on either side, facing the road, and also in some kind of barricade across the road we can build with cars and other stuff. If we triggered them at the right moment, they could literally kill hundreds of them all at once. I hope we don't ever have to, meaning I hope we never have to deal with a few hundred of them at the same time, but if we do … kaboom and done," he says with a sharp clap of his hands.

Morgan nods, mentally kissing the Corvette goodbye. They work their way through the rest of the locks, revealing more weapons than they can carry and some additional supplies, such as large jugs of water, dried beef jerky, batteries, flashlights, and camping gear. There's even a flamethrower tucked into a corner and attached to a backpack with a tank for the fuel all ready to go.

"Jesus," Bob marvels. "They were sure busy gathering all of this. I wonder if there is an armory near here, or a military base that they ransacked. That's a goddamn minigun of all things! We are *definitely* taking that. This isn't exactly over-the-counter stuff."

\*\*\*

Over the next couple of hours, they transfer the little bit of equipment and weapons they've brought with them from the car to the truck, and then load the truck's bed from the barn's supplies until it's almost creaking from the weight. They focus on the mines and a handful of automatic rifles from one of the deeper-in closets, plus the hand grenades, but it all weighs a ton once put together. Morgan's disappointed to lose the car that has taken her across the country, but she knows there will be plenty of dealerships to choose from once they reach the beach. For no particular reason, she tosses the car's key fob into the front seat. Maybe someone else will make use of it.

They climb into the truck, letting Jack have the entire rear seat to himself—he's happy to not be squeezed into the compact back area of the car again, even if he can't tell them so. They ease out of the barn, remembering to head toward the side road Chad took. Morgan's driving again since Bob remains a little groggy from the aftereffects of whatever drug he ingested, and just as she brings the truck into the sunlight, she notices something in the rearview mirror. She triggers the ignition off and hops out.

"What are you doing?" Bob asks. "Did you forget something?"

No reply.

Bob twists in his seat to see what she's doing and watches as Morgan crouches down in the center of the barn, looking at something that would have been right below where the truck was parked. Unable to see well enough from this angle, he, too, hops out and lets Jack's door open.

"What is it?" he asks.

"It's a trapdoor, but I'm not sure what it leads to."

And indeed there is. A poured concrete border smaller than the footprint of the truck is set into the floor of the garage, with a wooden door recessed within it that's the same color as the dirt. Morgan thinks about the ring from the bathroom and takes a deep breath. Chad and Daisy had wanted to capture more than kill her at first, and her mind races across the possibilities of what may be underneath the door, resurrecting her anger in a scarlet blossom of rage. It's time to listen again, but first, she calls Jack over and points down at the door, hoping for some kind of reaction. He walks onto the surface, his nails clicking on the wood, goes nose down for a second and then simply lopes away to jump back into the truck, nothing more than that. So no threat.

"Morgan, I don't know what might be under there, but I'm pretty sure of two things: I don't think I actually want to know, and whatever it might be, it's already over, or Jack would have reacted just now. We should leave it alone, we *really* should. There are some things that are better left unseen." Bob is practically pleading with her.

She stands, pensive and unhappy. He's probably right, but the part of her that had stood at the back of the women's support meetings in the past, listening to the stories being told and wanting to help those who couldn't help or defend themselves, really wants to open the door. Knowing the truth, no matter how terrible it may be, will always be better than spending the next however long having her mind come back to it. She knows if she doesn't look now, she'll be driving back here in a day or two, alone or with company;

there's no fighting her own unshakable will. Even she knows that—everyone else does too.

Bob takes her arm, gently, but it still makes her flinch as she's lost in her thoughts. "We should go and leave this place behind. You stopped them, we have more gear, and we have to finish the trip and check things out before everyone else gets here. Let it go. I know it's hard, but it's the smart thing to do."

She shakes her head, strands of hair made wild from the kitchen battle obscuring her face from view. There was a wide assortment of flashlights in Chad's equipment closets, so wordlessly, she grabs one of those and checks for battery power. After getting light, she goes over to the hatch, and when she senses Bob following, she waves an impatient hand at him to stay back. Not quite because she's angry at him, but perhaps because she's frustrated and understanding this needs to be a solo-Morgan moment, so she wants him away from her so she doesn't lash out.

Taking a deep breath, she holds the flashlight in one hand and grasps the silver half-moon hatch handle in the other. Jack's scratch and sniff had told her there's nothing dangerous down there, but she's still anxious as she lifts and points the light down into the recess now revealed. Six feet deep and as far across, and roughly eight feet long. Rough-finished cinder-block walls and a dirt floor.

Nothing.

Well, not exactly nothing. A small metal cot is tucked into one corner, the thin, dirty mattress halfway off it, with a ragged pillow and scrunched-up thin navy-blue blanket tossed indifferently on the floor. There's a small white plastic side table near the head of the bed, with a pink cup and bowl on it, both empty as far as she can tell.

Morgan stands, shining the light everywhere in the little alcove and looking again and again, as if she's going to see something new where there's no place to hide anything. More frustrated than before, now her imagination has to run amok at what might have happened here, and the anger returns with even greater power, surging through her arteries and muscles. For a moment or two, she imagines stalking back into the house and unleashing every single bullet they have into Chad and Daisy's bodies until they're unrecognizable jelly. Damn Chad for keeping his mouth shut, but in a way, she acknowledges that Bob is right—it's time to go.

Finally, without a word, she drops the hatch back down, walks back to the truck, restarts it, and starts to pull away.

"Morgan?"

"No ... just no."

The image of the space under the hatch filled with nothing and forlorn sadness at the same time follows her as she backs out of the driveway and back onto the road. She's pretty damn sure she'll have trouble ever shaking it from her memory; and she's right—not knowing the truth is indeed worse. *It's not fair*, she thinks in useless frustration. *We've always seen the face and nature of evil, even when it snuck up on us. I know the "who" but not the "what," and I hate it with every fiber of my being. Dammit!*

While the remainder of the drive is a picturesque one as the dense pines straddling the road slowly give way to marshland and the scrubby grasses and shrubs that could subsist in the briny tidewater and silty brown goo that passes for soil, the only one who notices any of these details is Bob. Morgan remains behind the wheel, which is good for her as it gives her something to do besides stew, and Jack sprawls happily across the rear seat. The new truck is pleasant enough to drive and has a full tank of gas, and the display tells her they have nearly 400 miles until empty, which is one less thing to worry about now. They're armed to the teeth, which is more important than they know, given what has happened to the rest of the group in New York.

# CHAPTER 10

Some road trips are better than others. I've always liked to drive, anywhere, starting with the euphoric freedom of it as a teenager sorting things out through my crappy daily commute to Charlotte and back in the more recent past. But today, I'm still angry and upset. We've been on the road for a lot of hours, largely in silence as we all absorb the triple whammy of losing Maya, losing a bunch of our gear—and not gaining anything new—and picking up Cody and Irish. Cody has been a bit on our shit list for trying to take down Morgan (and losing) and obviously is on Irish's as well. I'm not sure if Ajax keeps score like that or not, but he hasn't bitten Cody's face off yet so perhaps not … or maybe he's just waiting for a better time.

The truck feels full of the same uneasiness we had way back with not-the-dog Jack, when we had allowed him in the North Carolina house out of obligation to humanity, not because we wanted him there with us. That eventually turned out badly for Jack, but he had earned his outcome honestly, if you can put it that way. Cody apologized and all, but he bears watching, and I admit, I'm tired of not being able to trust newcomers. Or perhaps, tired of being proven over and over it's right to mistrust some of them.

Because of our later-than-planned start to the drive, we know we aren't going to make the full trip in a single, albeit long, day, so we haven't tried. Driving at night is a darker prospect than it was in the past since there's no residual light from mankind's creations, and of course, there are the roaming zombies who are too stupid to avoid moving vehicles to consider as well as the flourishing fauna that now wanders with abandon in these post-people days. It's a good rule of thumb to find somewhere remote with a good line of sight in all directions lit by the moon's glow, and we have done just that shortly after the day surrenders to the glooming shadows of late evening in southern Virginia. We post and rotate watches as always, now able to pair people up to ensure that if someone falls asleep, we'll still have some coverage. Standing guard in the dark, alone, is difficult since your body fights a battle of screamingly alert senses against ever-increasing fatigue brought on by silence, normal circadian rhythms, and a little helping of boredom.

After an uneventful night, we resume the trip the next day and soon cross the North Carolina to South Carolina state line, feeling the humidity increase as we continue on down I-95. While it has been the lingering tail end of summer in upstate New York and, therefore, very cool in the moonlit hours, it's much warmer here—the truck's outside temperature gauge says it's 92 degrees, and we feel all that and then some through the open windows. Normal people would have left their windows up and the air-conditioning on, but we're six humans and a dog who have just been in a little bit of a fight, two of us were stuck in a cozy armored personnel carrier for a while, and therefore, we all stink to high heaven. Showers are something of a relic of the past, though we'd all—minus Cody and Irish—bathed in the lake almost daily, but it has been an exciting couple of days, and we're a nose-wrinkling bunch and, hence, keep the windows open.

By my reckoning, we're only about three to four hours from meeting back up with Morgan and Bob. We lost our chance to collect any major weapons, but at least we've added a little to our collective firepower. I know Morgan's going to be upset by the loss of Maya and *thrilled* to see Cody again, so I feel some anxiety as we close in on our destination. We've been seeing signs for the Hilton Head exit for a bit, but I know, even once we turn off I-95, it'll take a while to cover the final southeastern stretch to the island. I'm at least relieved that aside from the wild start to the trip, it has been calm thereafter, and I hope it has been the same for Bob and Morgan.

# CHAPTER 11

They have howled through Bluffton on the approach to the causeway bridge leading from the mainland to the island—which kind of sounds like a song Jimmy Buffett should do: "From the main-land, to the eye-land …"—without seeing anything aside from humanity's leftovers. Not leftovers *of* people, but the leftovers *from* people. A road that had rarely seen a break in volume, no matter the time or season, is completely abandoned except for sporadic cars on the shoulders, but otherwise, it's a straight shot through at whatever speed Morgan chooses. The plan is to do a very quick recon of the island from end to end and then come back to wait for her brother and everyone else before deciding how to progress.

She slows the truck as they reach the bridge, and for a moment, she considers backing across it so if they run into trouble, she can bug out in a big hurry instead of trying a multipoint turnaround between the fairly snug concrete walls. No single 180-degree turn will be possible with the wide turn radius of the truck versus the Corvette, but she discards the idea of caution. Decades of jump first and figure it out second is hard to overcome, even when the "figure it out second" part tends to include battles to the death instead of thrill-seeking things, like jumping out of a perfectly good airplane or off a satisfactory and stable bridge while attached to a bungee cord.

Bob's scanning the crossing, looking for where he can create choke points and barriers, assuming the island is where they're going to land. For all they know, there could be a thousand monsters on that end of the bridge who haven't figured out how to get *off* the island and are just milling around and waiting for them, but the fact that they haven't seen any at all in this last hour is encouraging. The bridge leapfrogs from the mainland to a small island that won't serve any purpose for them, and then it takes a longer and higher jump to Hilton Head. It makes sense to put something at the peak of the bridge for the best visibility and then another, lower, string of obstacles a dozen yards ahead of that in order to slow down any assault.

*Finding suitable stuff for a barricade won't be a problem on an island of this size*, Bob thinks as they come around a gentle curve in the road and see someone has beaten them to the punch on that.

At first, it's hard to tell if the pile of debris across the bridge is intentional or accidental. Burned-out shells of cars and trucks are strewn across the space, and partially melted tires litter the area. There's nothing still burning, but whatever had has done so fiercely. The concrete of the road and sidewalls are scorched black for twenty yards ahead of the cars, and as they coast to a stop, they're able to see dozens of blackened, shrunken-into-fetal-position corpses mingled between the vehicles and random chunks of metal sprawled in their path. Whatever fight that occurred here had been a flat-out nasty brawl, but it's hard to tell who won, if anyone did. Like all battles back to the beginning of time, the dead always lost no matter what side they were on.

Morgan comes to a full stop and then climbs out. The separate but parallel bridge that's for traffic heading off the island has a pile of crushed cars in the same location; aside from being flat, they're otherwise undamaged, which means the pileup in front of them is intentional. Someone had built both, and then a fight broke out—there's no way to tell between who and what since a burned body looks the same whether it had started as a zombie or not, but the logical assumption is someone had the same thought as them: build a defensible wall across a choke point leading to an isolated and inaccessible place the zombies can't reach since they can't swim. Or can't as far as they know— there have been other surprises along the way where they had underestimated the monsters, but if this doesn't work, they'll be looking for a giant boat to live on or say, "Fuck it, let's fight until everyone or everything is dead." So there are most likely people on the island and, based on the panorama facing them, no monsters. Probably good signs, but it also means the truck goes no farther today, and they're going to be on foot for any recon.

Morgan turns the truck around, parking it in the middle of the road and leaving the key in the center console so if something happens, and only one of them gets back here, they'll be able to escape. They arm themselves carefully—weapons are heavy and awkward to run with, and speed is important. However, being caught by critters without enough weapons is right up there as a major problem, too, so they each carry an automatic rifle, a pistol, and a good measure of ammunition for each. Morgan also brings her Bo and machete. If it turns into a footrace, they can toss the guns and haul ass. Morgan is conscious she can run far faster than Bob given her youth, her athleticism, and his Achilles injury, and she hopes she won't have to face a decision of any kind about leaving him behind, but living for everyone else is paramount, no matter how much she likes him. Hopefully, that's something she won't have to worry about.

All the blackened detritus is cool to the touch, telling a story of an old fight, like the litter of the Second World War still visible in Europe. They study the stack of cars that looms about twelve feet high from the road without seeing a path of hand- and footholds they're both capable of climbing. Morgan goes back to the truck and backs it up tight to the barricade, and they step onto the edge of the bed for a head start. She sees her route clearly enough now and points it out to Bob.

"I don't think I can do that," he says quietly, slightly turning his face away from her. "It's tough for me to pull my weight up with my arms and shoulders and drive off my feet. I'm just not as strong as I was, and that asshole Marcus cutting my Achilles tendon so I couldn't escape robbed my legs of their strength to compensate. You go. I'll stay here and guard our back."

She can tell he's extremely unhappy to have to admit all that, though she's glad he feels comfortable enough with her to do so. Most people are intimidated by her physicality and try to match it (always unsuccessfully), and she's used to that. Morgan thinks about splitting up; she'll be fine on her own, and he can see a long way from where the truck is parked, but she decides they should stick together. If something happens, he would literally be trapped with his back against the wall, truckload of guns notwithstanding.

After scanning the wreckage again, she sees an option. "I tell you what. See that side-view mirror there, up on the silver whatever-it-was?" she says, pointing upward. "If I can get you up to there, you should be able to get to the top on your own. It means I'm going to have to give you a big boost. You're going to have to stand on my knees and step to my shoulders, and then I'm going to hold you steady until you're on the mirror. I'm not going to tell anyone, okay?"

He looks at her with a dose of gratitude clear in his eyes and simply nods at first but then asks, "What are we going to do when we get to the top? How are we … or really, how am I going to get down?"

What-ifs and how-can-we's simply never occur to Morgan. Thinking far ahead takes the fun out of it, whatever "it" happens to be at the time. You just do the next thing in front of you and figure it out along the way. That approach has worked out fine for a long time, so at first, she can't understand why Bob is even asking, but then she replies once she realizes that getting off the pile of cars is going to be the same on the far side. "We'll figure it out when we get up there. I can climb down for sure, and then I'll get you off the top, too, somehow. Don't worry about it."

After letting her get her feet well set, Bob uses Morgan as a human ladder, scuffling his way up the stack of wrecks and clambering to stand atop the pile. "Hey, we're going to be fine. There's a platform on the back. Come on up."

She reaches their weapons up and then climbs quickly, using her hands and feet in tandem and joins him, standing on the roof of what had been a large SUV and is now about a fourth of its prior size. On the reverse side of the barricade are a pair of the industrial rolling staircases that were common in the home improvement stores of yore—silver with holes circled by gripping edges in the stairs and a small three-foot-square top platform. They face outside in. The stairs begin on the outsides of the bridge so the platforms are close to one another in the middle, and the span between the two is about six feet across. That's bridged by a wooden scaffold of two-by-fours, leaving an observation post that can accommodate four or perhaps five people in a pinch. The view back the way they have traveled is still vacant, and they turn around to face the declining slope of the bridge leading the rest of the way to the island. More scattered, blackened debris, a pair of dead (normal human) bodies lying awkwardly at the foot of the wall—those people clearly fell or jumped off and landed badly. There's a bright-red golf cart facing the island a dozen yards away, with a white-bordered roof wrapped around silvery panels between the edges and no golf bag in the back—instead, there's a cardboard tube strapped where the golf clubs would have been, and it's filled with a motley assortment of rifles.

Climbing down, they go to investigate. Boxes of ammunition fill the small basket between the seating area and club storage that's now for guns, and the key is in the ignition.

"Those are solar panels on the roof," Bob says. "Someone rigged them up since you can see the ragged cuts made by whoever did it to remove the plastic roof. Clever, and should be ready to go. Let me drive this time, okay?"

"Sure. This is more your speed anyway, old man. I don't care how well you handled the Corvette, you're, like, ten minutes from being in a wheelchair or walker, so this is a good transition for you. Just take it easy and don't floor it."

"You're such a shit, you know that?"

Morgan's reluctant to leave their gear and the dog in the truck, but there's nothing for it. Getting it over the wall is a problem for later, but she figures they'll sort that out. Maybe they can find a working powerboat or a rowboat big enough to hold the gear in only a few trips. The distance between the mainland and island is no small gap for someone rowing; it's going to be a serious workout, even if the water is still, so she hopes for the best.

They arrange their own weapons and get in the golf cart. Then Bob turns to her. "Shall we?"

"Yep, I guess so. Keep your eyes peeled since this thing is barely going to be faster than a jog, so if we run into trouble, we're probably better getting out and hauling ass on foot."

Bob turns the key, which, of course, makes no noise in a golf cart, and stomps on the gas. Surprisingly, it's a fast golf cart. Not *fast*, but fast enough that it will actually outrun a speedy person. "Someone tinkered with the engine, too, it looks. This is fun, but it's going to take a while to really get anywhere. This is a big island. You should hold on tight."

"Why do I need to hold on? I'm a big girl."

"Because you're a big girl with a smart mouth who is disrespectful to her elders, and I might push you out when you're not looking."

They laugh, feeling at ease now that the first phase of the trip is over, and head down the hill to see what waits for them in the tourist paradise.

"What do you think happened back there?" Morgan asks.

"I don't know for sure," Bob answers. "Beyond the obvious of the barricade, then some kind of battle, the defenders either set fire to something or made a mistake. It's hard to tell. I guess it's a good sign, though, that the stack of cars is intact. Assuming it was zombies attacking, they didn't get over it as far as we can see, so we can use it too. I already have some ideas about how to make it better, especially since we have all those claymore mines and the nasty minigun, thanks to our dead friends. A good start anyway."

They reach the island itself, grinning at the Welcome sign at the foot of the bridge and seeing nothing threatening so far. Hilton Head is shaped like a foot, a large foot, and the first few miles on-island—going from the ankle to heel—aren't particularly interesting other than a tease of, "Are we there yet?" and "Yes, but wait another fifteen minutes until we're there-there," for countless tourists carting small kids with them in the past. It wouldn't have been uncommon for inbound traffic to be going as slowly as they are since check-in time had been the same for everyone and resulted in thousands arriving all at once, but having the road entirely to themselves *and* only going twenty mph is an odd feeling. It's a beautiful, sunny, not-terribly-humid-or-cloudy day that's utterly silent. They see no signs of life (or nonlife) as they drive for another thirty minutes and reach what would have been the more heavily populated areas.

Nothing.

"This is weird. I don't like it much," Morgan says, breaking the monotonous hum of the golf cart. "Where did whoever was here go? Are they all dead?"

"I don't know, but I don't care for it either. I think we should turn around now that we've seen a bit at least. Seems safe enough, and this is taking forever. Thinking we should go wait for everyone else and maybe look for a working pontoon boat or similar back on shore that'll make it easier to get our gear across, or maybe a hardware store to grab a ladder or two. Once we get the rest here, we can all recon once we find an actual motor vehicle that covers ground faster. Maybe not, but this is a darn big island. There has to be *something* we can use."

Morgan nods in agreement, and so Bob swings the cart around and drives back to the bridge. They park at the foot of the barrier and climb back up the staircases, wondering if there's anything naughty waiting for them on the other side.

Nothing.

They climb down carefully, hop back in the truck, apologize to Jack for leaving him, cross over to town, and go shopping. There aren't any of the stores Bob wants on the main drag, but they have time and keep searching. Finally coming to a home improvement store one road in from the main drag and finding the items Bob has in mind, they gather all those up, stack them on top of the weapons and ammo, and head back to the beginning of the bridge. To wait for everyone else.

# CHAPTER 12

We leave the interstate and begin the final stretch of eastbound travel. The air picks up the faint sulfur stench of the low-country marshlands, even though none of those are in sight at the moment. One of the biggest subtle changes in the absence of most of humanity is the olfactory and auditory clutter we'd all been accustomed to—car noise and exhaust more than anything else as people needed to get somewhere other than where they were, but ordinary background sounds like lawns being mowed, planes overhead, the clatter of people on their phones and all the other noise of the world is gone. It used to amaze me when I awoke early—like, stupid early, as in 4 a.m. or earlier—on weekends and sat outside on the back porch, sipping coffee, that there was a constant white noise audible, even a handful of miles removed from the highway. Where the phrase "silence is golden" comes from, I have no idea since I don't think anyone *really* knows what silence sounds like. We do now, even though, at the moment, we're making noise of our own in the truck.

Everyone has been quiet for a while now, either lost in their thoughts or dozing. I'm anxious to reach Bluffton and regroup with Bob and Morgan. Eve said a while back that she hopes they're okay; I have no real concern about that since Morgan seems to come out of any scrapes unscathed while whoever's on the other side of the conflict goes home with their tail between their legs, but I'm looking forward to restoring the full group. Minus Maya, dammit.

There's a certain stoic majesty to bridges that cross larger spans. They stand there, simple and usually not aesthetically pleasing other than their symmetry of form, proudly carrying us from one side to another without complaint. I get the sense that all of them will be standing long after we're gone, waiting to connect one thing to another, to do their job. It's like the people who had worked in countless offices across the world—they were always there, doing their job, not spectacular, not special, but always present and capable; the backbones of their companies. Not the executives or owners, but the people who did the stuff that made it all work, rarely being noticed until they were gone. That was the part of society that had made the Trench Monkeys famous, singing about the regular people and their regular problems. The infrastructure of the country is the same way—you use it and barely notice it unless there's a problem. This bridge is hopefully going to be a passage and a solution. We see it stretching ahead and leading to what we hope is a new sanctuary before catching sight of the black pickup in the middle of the road.

We've been looking for the blazing-red Corvette, of course, and I come alert when I see motion near the bed of the truck, human (or not) near the rear and away from us. At first, I back off the gas and subconsciously reach for my ever-present .45, and then Morgan comes into full view. I smile and speed up to cross the last few hundred yards and then turn the truck off. Everyone spills out, with Ajax and Jack greeting one another like a couple of giddy kids who haven't seen each other in years versus days, and the two of them lope off to find some grass to water or fertilize.

Introductions are made all around as we all speak happily, glad to be off the road and back together. Morgan smirks when she sees Cody, clearly recalling their early-morning first meeting, but she's pleasant enough to him and Irish.

"Where is Maya?" she asks me after a minute or two, brow furrowed.

"Let's walk off for a minute," I say and take her arm to steer her away from the group.

She tenses at first when I do but then relaxes. Morgan isn't used to anyone moving her anywhere she hadn't already been planning on going, and I'm the only exception that I know of—the rest of humanity has been held at a disdainful arm's length by my sister for most of her life.

I fill her in on everything that has happened—the discovery of the remnants of the army camp, Maya's death, our rescue of Irish and Cody, and then scrambling away just in time from the thousands of zombies.

"Thousands? Are you sure?"

"It was a freaking wave of them. So, yeah, thousands of them chasing us. And they were fast. They nearly caught Ajax."

"That's not good, but at least they're hundreds of miles away, so it's not like they can follow us here or anything. We should be good here. Wait'll you see the bridge and hear what Bob has cooked up," she says with a grin.

"Did you guys get along okay on the drive?" I ask since it isn't always ideal for her to be closed up with another person in a small space for too long. More accurately, it isn't usually good for the other person.

"We hit a bump or two at first, but we're good now. He's not so bad, and pretty smart too," she answers. "He made me take a look at things maybe a little differently," she adds without elaborating further. Then she fills me in on their detour with Chad and Daisy.

"Jesus. What the fuck is wrong with people?" That's a trick question—there's a *lot* wrong with people, even before the rules died along with the humans, and as we've found out, not all the survivors are good guys, so there's still plenty of "wrong" to go around. "At least you picked up some new toys out of it."

"True. Those are going to be helpful if we need them. And you found some new people, so the beginning and middle of the trips were good for something, I guess. I'd like to shoot for boring now that we're here though." Morgan pauses, takes a slow breath, and lets it out with something of a sigh. "I'm going to miss Maya," she continues with a little slump in her shoulders. "She was just mellow and easy to be around, which I can't say about everyone. She would have been really happy here at the beach too. That was shitty luck. Let's go back though. It's getting late, and we should get over the wall before dark since we're going to be on foot."

"The wall?"

"You'll see."

*

It's a pain in the ass getting over the wreckage that blocks access to the island, though one of the things Bob and Morgan have brought back with them after shopping is a ladder. One of the other things is a welding unit—a torch, tanks, and a mask. The tanks are miserably heavy, and I'm not looking forward to getting those up and over, even with help, but Bob says to leave them on the near side anyway.

We park both vehicles facing away from the wall so if push comes to haul ass, they're ready to go. I leave my key above the sun visor, and Morgan leaves her own key fob in the center console. We've parked them in a staggered pattern so anything coming toward us in a wave will have to slow down into three bottlenecks—one on each side of the trucks and between those and the concrete side barriers, and one between the trucks themselves.

The sun is steadily getting lower, so we hurry as much as we can to haul all the gear from the vehicles up and over the stack of cars. It takes us well over an hour, and at the end, I have to ungracefully grab each of the (damn heavy) dogs, put them over my shoulder, and hand them up to the others without falling off the ladder. The dogs like it about as much as I do, whining uneasily as we ascend, but it beats the shit out of swimming, and I tell them so.

I pause at the top of the fighting platform, look back to where we've been, and see nothing but a magnificent southern sunset, colors painting the clouds in a swirling pink, orange, and yellow canvas of solace. *I hope that's going to hold true*, I think and struggle to lift the ladder up vertically over the wall so no one else can follow us easily.

"We sleep here for tonight. Two guards. I'll go first, and, Irish, why don't you join me?"

I'd been thinking while we were moving all the weapons and other gear that I want two guards on this wall at all times, regardless of where we settle. Given a choice, I know everyone will want to be on the beach, and I've been thinking about the only large hotel I know of on the beach itself: a hulking, ugly concrete monolith that sits sulking on the waterfront in one of the segments Hilton Head is broken up into, around mid-island. Ugly or not, it's big, and if I remember right, it's at least fifteen stories tall with a great line of sight in all directions and, therefore, more defendable than one of the gorgeous but comparatively small adjacent houses on the water. We'll see, but anyway, that hotel is a solid ten-minute drive from where we are, so two guards to keep one another awake and company; one of whom can hop in a vehicle and come to get help if needed. Maybe we'll do three. Something to decide, though there aren't that many of us to spare for guard duty: me, Morgan, Bob, Eve, Kuniko, Amy, Irish, Cody, and the dogs. And dogs can't drive. Eight people, four pairs, rotating in shifts of six hours … doesn't sound like a lot of fun, but we haven't lived this long by ignoring the necessities. We'll probably need to mix who's on guard as well so no one gets on anyone else's nerves, but the pairings have to be well thought out. Setting Eve and Amy together, for example, won't be much firepower, but we'll have to continue training everyone for reality. Those two *have* to get more comfortable pulling the trigger, or it'll come back to bite us at some point.

*Oh, I see what you did there. Ha. I also see that a change of location hasn't improved your choice of words. Sigh. At least it's warmer here, I'll give you that.*

Irish moves over toward me while everyone else makes their way down the steps to do their best to settle in for the night. "Sure, us army folk're good for standing watch. We've got a night-vision set, so as long as those batteries last, we should use them but not all the time, just if we hear something or see motion and need a closer look at it."

"Sounds good. We need to keep an eye out in both directions tonight. Morgan said they drove for about a half hour without seeing anything, but you never know." I pause for a minute while the group moves farther out of earshot. "What's your take on Cody?" I ask her, wanting to get another opinion, especially from someone who was around him previously. In that, I'm disappointed.

"I don't know him much, to be honest. Cody and a handful of others were the long-range patrol guys, the ones who would go out on foot and run ahead of the larger groups as silent scouts when we were on the move or for perimeter security when we were sitting still. They were all runners and kind of solitary, keeping to themselves. Never heard anyone say anything bad about him back on base. Never heard anyone say anything good either though."

Great. Right where I was three minutes ago. "What do you think now, after what happened?" Women always seem to have better sense for this stuff than men, and God knows I've made some judgment errors when it came to character over the past couple of years.

I can barely see her face in the darkening evening. Light kind of winks out these days without the ambient glow from something man-made. One minute, it's still a tiny bit light, the next, it's as dark as the moon's cycle allows. "I think he's okay. Thought he was telling the truth about being scared and freaking out, though those guys should've been trained out of being nervous. But you know, you were there too. That was an absolute shitload of zombies, and they'd had their way with us professional soldiers not too long before and were coming back for seconds. Pretty normal to be afraid. I sure was …." She trails off, probably recalling the initial assault by the monsters.

I think for a minute or two, balancing what she's said against what I've seen as well as the history of my group. If I'm wrong again, someone's going to be pissed with me, but then again, I would be too. I decide we'll give him a shot, and then if it doesn't work, even a little, we'll give him a *shot*. "I agree with you, I think. Let's be careful. Can you be keeping an eye on him and come talk to me or Morgan if anything looks or feels wrong? We'll have to be thoughtful about sentry combinations, too, until enough time has passed to feel better, or not."

I sense more than see her nod in the dark. "You're the boss."

"I don't know about that. None of us are the boss."

"Stop kidding yourself. I've been in the military for over five years, and there are people who are assigned the title, and those who just bring it with them. You're one of those. Everyone looks to you, I can see that already. And they're right."

I hope she's right ... I hope they all are.

# CHAPTER 13

Night One is quiet. And hot. And humid. Irish and I stand guard for a handful of hours until Morgan wakes up and nudges Amy to join her and replace us. I rest fitfully until daylight since my brain is running ahead to all the tasks we have ahead of us, like transportation now that the trucks are stuck on the far side of the wall, and where to live, and more food, and scouring the island clean. There have to be zombies here, even though the walls on the bridge block it off from the mainland. The odds scream against us that these walls were built in time to prevent an invasion in the very earliest days, and there hadn't already been zombies on-island, but we'll find out.

Hilton Head is a big island. Without a car or truck, it's a *huge* island. Job number one is to find something bigger and better than the golf cart Bob and Morgan found, no matter how extra-quick it can go. Eight people plus two dogs plus all our crap—though, a lot of weapons are going to be left right here—will take forever to move to the hotel, so Eve and Kuniko leave in the cart to hunt down something that will start.

Morgan, Irish, and Cody work to sort out the combined guns and ammunition we all carry to add to their haul, organizing everything on the surface of the road so the ammo is matched to its guns, and we can then divide it all up.

Amy and I stand watch, though I let her doze off since she's beat, and it's daylight. Bob found a pair of binoculars back at Chad's place, and I use those to scan in every direction often, certain I'm going to see some wave of zombies on their way, but I'm more looking for individuals that will be harder to notice than a moving group.

Bob is on the far side of our wall with the welding gear and tanks. What he's doing isn't immediately obvious, but after a few minutes of watching him cut slivers of sheet metal off the flattened cars and trucks that make up the barricade and weld them back to the wall in razor-sharp spikes pointed slightly down toward the concrete surface of the bridge, I figure it out. Besides making the wall look like a metal hedgehog, the angled-down pieces won't allow anyone or anything to climb the spikes since feet or hands will slip off even if the climber somehow manages to not shred their hands on the intentionally jagged cuts in the attempt. It isn't long before Bob's shirt is soaked by the combo of the day's escalating temperature and heat from the torch, but he's making a formidable addition to our defenses.

The guns group finishes their tasks and moves on to the rest of our supplies and sorts those as well, and then they try to cool off as they stand with hands on hips or knees. It's *hot*, even though it has to be fall.

That's one of the tricks of the new world. I have no idea what day, month, or even year it is since I haven't been counting along the way and have long discarded my watch because there's no practical use for it any longer and reflected sun from the face could alert monsters to my location, so I had tossed it. Is it August? September? No idea, but it had been getting steadily colder in New York, so I guess we're in the latter part of September, which means it'll be hottish for another month here. People had been so regimented in the past, always going somewhere to be "on time," and now we're firmly off time. You eat when hungry—which is often during these lean days—sleep when tired, and generally follow the cycle of Earth. Not much point in staying up late anymore unless on guard since all the lights are off. One benefit to all this is I don't have to keep track of daylight savings time anymore.

Our instinctive sense of time, however, is as sharp as can be, and I realize Eve and Kuniko have been gone for longer than I like, and so I turn my focus to the island's broad swathe of tree cover. It's unlike most of the other coastal islands I've visited in the Carolinas in that it's far more lush, almost tropical, instead of a sandy bump that just happens to be big enough to build houses on. The trees, laced with Spanish moss, cover a large chunk of the island's surface and arch over many of the side roads. That's nice when you need some shade, but it's a pain in the ass right now when I need a good line of sight. Nothing in view to my bare eyes, and the binoculars aren't any help either, and I feel myself getting restless. I'm not prepared to lose anyone else, especially Eve since we have unfinished business of a sort. Not "business" like *that* "business." Well, maybe *that* "business" too. *If she's lucky,* I think, joking with myself and then feeling silly mixed with a small side order of shame for it.

*Hey! You're just a moron. You shouldn't feel silly or ashamed though, just stupid.*

Well, look who's here.

*Did you miss me?*

Not really, no.

*So here we go again. Someone needs to keep you straight.*

Okay then, I'll play. What do you mean?

*Guilty for wanting Eve? You've been a puppy about her for forever, right? And she likes you, that's obvious, too, but she's on a different clock than you are. Girls are weird. That was true in elementary school and still is when you're "grown-ups." And yeah, I did just do the air quotes with my nonexistent fingers thing.*

*You shouldn't feel bad for thinking about her in any way you want. Inside your head is about the only safe place left on the planet. Everyone,* everyone *on Earth had thoughts they wouldn't be proud to tell their mom, even the sanctimonious assholes who liked to dig up tweets or posts or whatever else from ten years back when someone became newly famous in order to knock them down so they could hold themselves up instead as glowing examples of human behavior. All those holier-than-thou clowns had a questionable bit of clutter in their mental closets, too, just were smart enough to keep their fingers off the keyboard or touchscreen.*

Um, who are you, how did you get in my head, and where did the "real" you go? And yeah, I just did the air quotes thing with my actual fingers.

"Are you okay?" asks Amy sleepily.

I glance down to see her with one eye open, looking at me as if I've lost my mind, and I can't help but chuckle. "Yeah, I'm fine, just having a little conversation with myself. You ever do that?"

"Um, no," she answers with a small eye roll and then lays her head back down.

*Don't be a dick. I'm trying to help you. I always try to help you, but you don't listen closely enough. Shoot Jack, don't trust Ned, and so on. And what do you do? You run and hide in a closet in the basement that has no door when the bad guy is chasing you with a chain saw. Pay attention.*

*What you and lots of people fell for was that "they" managed to make everyone feel guilty for being human. People think and do all kinds of crazy shit. It's part of the charm. Squirrels are boring. They all look the same and do the same thing. Fish ... are those really all that interesting? But people, you all are as much fun as a bag full of cats and catnip. Sure, some bad apples are out there who aren't wired right and make everyone else look bad, but the variety of people is what makes it all great and sad and crazy and fun and whatever else.*

*Back to "they." That group wanted to neuter everyone, dumb them down, make the world a giant flock of sheep waiting for someone to tell them what to do, saying this was okay and that was not because it sounded like actual fun. Your colonel back in New York might have gotten carried away just a teeny, tiny bit with killing billions, but some of his ideas were legit. The world was filling up with drones addicted to a little glass screen one foot from their face, seeing what someone else decided they should see thanks to algorithms and advertising dollars, and not looking out at the magnificence of the world. How many do you think died without even looking up?*

You've got a point in here somewhere that's relevant to what I've been thinking about, right?

*Yes. It's simple: be a human. Be a hu*man. *Eat meat, mow the grass with your shirt off, even if you could stand a few sit-ups, cheer your sports team on like a lunatic, drink too much sometimes, think about sex with a pretty girl and be happy about it, shoot the fucking zombies, all that good stuff. Speaking of … heads up, something interesting is* finally *going to happen.*

I look up, not noticing until now that I've been absently staring at the water off the edge of the bridge, and there, as promised, is something interesting. Eve and Kuniko are racing toward the wall—if "racing" is an accurate word when speeding in a golf cart—and waving their arms. I hold my spot and lift the binoculars up to watch the road behind them.

Zombies, a bunch of them, run-jogging steadily in our direction. More than I can count easily, so I visually cut them in half and then again, count that group and multiply by four to get about sixty of them. Sixty is a bad number; more than we've ever fought en masse, not counting the horde that had chased us back at the army camp or the one at Marcus's compound, where mostly what we did was run away.

*This is one of those times to be a man. Kick some ass, a lot of it, fight for your people, and then one of these days, walk over there and kiss the girl. Not like a caveman, but let's say politely. Chances are good she's going to kiss you back. And if she doesn't, say you're sorry and move on. Not like you're going to get crucified for trying. All the people who would have happily strung you and anyone else up for doing that are deader than the crowd stomping your way. They're simple. They want to kill everyone, not just whoever is out of fashion at the moment.*

I guess I should say thanks for the pep talk? I actually mean it though—you're right on a couple of points at least, so thanks. I admit, I'm coming around to the new you.

*You're welcome. And seriously, go kill all those fucking zombies. And remember, when you and Eve do eventually bump uglies, I'll be there, too, maybe with some more advice or criticism. Probably more of the latter, but don't let me stop you.*

And there he is.

I shout to everyone else to gear up as Eve coasts the cart to a stop and both of the women hop out in a hurry, running to the piles of guns and ammunition. This side of the wall is going to be a problem to defend—no spikes, no obstacles other than the golf cart, and while we could climb over and down (carefully) and take off in the trucks, we're going to be slow to do that. Eight people, two big dogs who are absolutely not going to be left behind, all our shit we need.

Everyone looks to me. I guess I am indeed the boss.

*Don't let it go to your head.*

"We fight! There are a lot of us, and we have enough guns, and they're at least going to be pretty close together as they approach thanks to the bridge, so it'll be hard to miss."

Fear on a few faces, resignation on others, joy on Morgan's.

"Amy, Kuniko, Eve, all up on the step stairs. Hey, Irish and Cody, who's the better shot?"

"Probably Cody," Irish replies, her voice clipped and strong—the voice of someone used to being in a fight as part of her job. "He was in the field more."

"Cody, hop up there on the ladders, too, with one of the rifles and see if you can whittle them down a bunch as they approach."

Everyone gets moving, with the three women grabbing pistols and clattering up the metal steps of the ladders. Pistols make sense for them since they're the least experienced with weapons, and if or when the fighting gets this close, the poor accuracy of a handgun won't be as noticeable. Basically, if the zombies make it all the way to the steps, we're in a ton of trouble, but they'll be able to choose targets at their feet not more than a few yards away. Morgan has her Bo, the machete, a shotgun, and Jack sitting beside her. It's hard to tell whose gaze is more intense, hers or the dog's, but they both look at ease despite being outnumbered by seven to one. Ajax has trotted over to me, and Bob clambers up the ladder from his welding work, picks up a rifle, and stands waiting, his nerves betrayed by his glances in every direction. Irish hefts her automatic rifle, checks the clip for ammo, pats her chest once, lifts a finger and her eyes to the sky, and sights down the barrel toward our enemies as naturally as can be. Rock steady.

I check my KNIFE, the ever-present and trusty .45s I have tucked at my waist, another automatic rifle from the stash Morgan and Bob have collected, and a handful of grenades since I have the best arm in the group. It has been a little while since we've been in a brawl, and I steady my breathing though feel my pulse rate pick up in anticipation. One of the thoughts I keep inside my head is that even though it comes with fear, I enjoy this, too, like Morgan does. There's freedom in this—me against you, everyone bring their best fastball, and let's find out who wins.

*That's the spirit.*

Four of us on the ground with the dogs, evenly spaced across the bridge with me and Morgan in the center, and the other four up high on the stairs, all watching the monsters come to visit. I wish we had time to set the minigun up, but we'll have to make do.

"Light 'em up!" I roar, feeling adrenaline surge throughout my body. It's everything I can do to wait instead of racing toward them, to take a toll in blood.

Cody fires first, not on full automatic but in controlled three-shot bursts, methodically working his way from the center of the mass coming toward us so to ensure maximum effect, and I see a handful of them fall and be trod over by the following waves. Irish adds her rifle to the cacophony, and more of them drop. I pull the pin from a grenade and throw it as far as I can, watching as it strikes the surface in front of the mass of monsters, bounces high in the air, and tumbles before exploding. The effect is awesome, shredding heads, torsos, and limbs, and they're down at least a dozen by now, the blood of the fallen drizzling back toward the island as the remaining ones continue their ascent of the bridge. Maybe seventy yards away now.

It's a slaughter. Bob joins in, screaming as he fires, and he and Irish keep shooting while I lob another pair of grenades into the crowd, this time as they get closer, taking a horrible toll on them. Horrible if you're on their side anyway. Blood splashes in every direction to stain the road and sidewalls a dripping scarlet, and their battle cry finally comes, though weaker than it would have been a few moments ago.

*Muuuuuuuhhhhh!*

The remaining fifteen or so race toward us, some of them stumbling over the fallen or on damaged limbs of their own.

I haven't used the pistols yet, and my rifle is also unused. Morgan, too, has refrained from firing her weapon, just watches as the bodies fall, her face implacable. She glances at me and pointedly crouches to rest her shotgun on the ground, flicking the Bo up and around to rest like a walking stick in front of her. A raised eyebrow and nod of her head toward the remnants rushing our way.

"It's too many, Morgan," I say, knowing what she has in mind.

She'd told me about her hunting in Denver in the early days, patrolling the city each day for crowds of zombies to kill, in some cases without firearms. Just like her to push the limits, and just like her to drag me into it.

"Not for long it won't be," she says as she unwinds the hair band all women with long hair seem to always have on their wrists, and she ties her hair up and out of the way. "So, wanna race?"

I nod back. I'm not as reckless as she's going to be, so I let go of my rifle and haul out the pair of pistols. I reach down and pat Ajax on his big noggin. "Come if you want to, big boy."

We charge, the dogs immediately at our heels, though they could have easily outrun us. The zombies seem to hesitate for just a heartbeat in surprise but then close the remaining distance quickly. I fire as I run, taking four of them down before we close ranks and smash together. Morgan belts one in the face, crumpling its nose and spilling teeth from a broken jaw with a nasty overhead blow from her Bo and moves to strike the next one's knees before the first one hits the ground. She wades in like she was born to do this, and perhaps she was.

I slip one pistol back in at my waist to trade for the KNIFE and fire in one direction while slashing in another. I cut across a female's face, right above her eyebrows, and a sheet of blood erupts to blind her. Ajax takes her down, grabbing an ankle in his massive jaw with a thick *crunch*, and drags her to the ground. When he dips his dripping maw toward her neck, I look up and away—some things don't need to be seen in all their detail. He, too, is doing what he's supposed to do, and it isn't guard houses or go for a jog in the park.

It's all a blur, though it feels choreographed in a way. We've fought against them so many times that everything except for us moves more slowly, letting me see what's going to happen, as if unfolding in slow motion, like a movie running at the wrong speed. I glimpse Morgan cracking her wooden staff across the clawing arms reaching for her before she finally lets go, drawing her machete as the battle closes in tight. I realize everyone else has stopped shooting, which makes sense, of course, I just haven't noticed the absence of the gunfire. Lifting the pistol in my left hand, I spin and fire through faces and torsos, watching the gore spray out in a funnel to paint their compatriots crimson. Too close in now, so I focus on the blade of the KNIFE, slashing as hungry mouths lunge at me, broken teeth looming for a bite, chomping together with a sound like a stapler on speed. I hold one scrawny but wiry-strong male by the neck in one hand while I rip the gleaming blade through the throat of another, decapitating it in the single swipe. They're running out of full bodies now, but one of the wounded ones latches onto my ankle, pulling with their surprising strength to lift its torso up and get at me. I've dropped pistol two but haul one back out fast and fire down into its face, which explodes, raining bits and pieces in all directions.

*Click.*

No more bullets.

The hoarse bellows of rage from the two dogs now outweighs the zombies' groans and growls. Two of them left standing, lots of them down and unmoving, a couple handfuls crawling and dragging their way toward us over the

piles of bodies. I'm covered in blood, none of it mine as far as I can tell. I've been struck a few times by elbows or hands, but without weapons, they have a hard time injuring you in a hand-to-hand fight unless they can swarm you to the ground. I'll have a nice collection of bruises and scrapes, but I'm pretty used to those by now. Morgan stands right next to me, like she always has, breathing heavily and covered by an utterly disgusting mess of nastiness but with a huge grim smile on her face. I hear the blood drizzling off her right arm, down the blade of the machete, and onto the ground.

No one moves. The last two zombies simply stand there, shell-shocked maybe. Irish steps between us, rifle still at the ready.

"That was some crazy shit right there. Y'all just ran *toward* them. And then you two killed pretty much all of them without taking a scratch. I'm glad we're on the same team. We *are* on the same team, right?" she asks with a nervous grin.

Morgan laughs and pats her on the shoulder, leaving a bloody handprint on Irish's drab-green tank top. "Yeah, we are. Don't forget the dogs helped too. Take care of these last two, will you?"

The two shots echo over the peaceful water, followed by a dozen more as she walks through and eliminates the survivors with head shots.

Cody whoops in glee. "Did you fuckin' see that? We wasted them! Dozens of those stupid motherfuckers, and we killed them *all!*"

As he hollers, he turns and grabs Kuniko by the arms and pulls her in for a smooch right on the mouth. She pushes him away with an unhappy expression flickering across her face but doesn't make a big deal out of it. Everyone is smiling, mostly from relief. We haven't straight up fought a group that size before, and winning fairly easily gives us some confidence, though I take it with a mammoth grain of salt. Things aren't easy these days.

I look at my sister—nothing needs to be said between us. Again we've stood up, together, and come out on the other side just fine. She nods at me once more, and we walk by ourselves slowly down the bridge toward the island, avoiding the rivers of zombie blood that trickle alongside. There isn't anything else to fight, but we need a bath, and I whistle the dogs to us since they're gross too.

Everyone else watches us go.

***

Once the two of us scrub all the zombie goo off ourselves and scour the dogs in the shallows near the foot of the bridge, we come back up the rise of the span to find everyone else busying themselves with cleaning up the mess. Dispensing with zombie corpses is grisly work since they're … well, disgusting. They've been deteriorating over time, now skinnier, less dressed, and more rotten than they had been in the beginning. I get a sense they're winding down in a way, which is possible since their food supplies have to be dwindling. Not many people left, and most of the remaining animals are more agile than they are, or can climb or fly, and they aren't going to go hit the grocery store exactly. I wonder if we can simply wait them out, if we can hold on for a year or two more, if they'll just run out of steam, and we'll be truly alone in the wide world. And safe. It's good to want things, and luck is in generally short supply, so we're going to make a big bad wall even nastier and then watch over it.

As I drag one toward the side of the road, it's foot simply comes off in my hand. I toss it away over the side toward the water in surprise and disgust. A buzzard from the pack circling lazily overhead in the heat loops down quickly to snag it in midair, but then it drops it immediately, finding it not to his liking. Can't say I blame him, but I think it's interesting a carrion eater is declining to eat another.

At first, Cody had suggested we toss them all over the edge of the bridge down into the river, but I disagreed with that. Why contaminate the water, even though it isn't drinking water? The medieval part of me wants to cut their heads off and mount those on Bob's new skewers jutting from the far side of the wall as a warning to others, but I discard that idea as gross (like the foot), as too much work, and out of doubt that zombies give a shit that we've killed a bunch of them.

I'll be wrong about that last one.

Without access to the trucks as hearses, we drag and stack the bodies like firewood about one hundred yards downhill from the wall, tight against the concrete sidewall of the bridge to be well out of the way. Luckily, the breeze is steady here all the time, and I hope for rain to wash things off. I try not to look too closely at the pile of former humans—it's always easy to hate the monsters and forget they have all been moms, dads, kids, whatevers beforehand with a normal life (whatever counts as "normal") until being turned into killing machines against their will. Reminded of that, I say a silent prayer for their peace now.

Once we're finished, Cody climbs back onto the stairs to keep watch while the rest of us take a break for food and drink.

"We need to get off the bridge soon," Bob says, sitting cross-legged next to Kuniko, who nods in agreement. "If there are more of them on the island side, or more than just came for us, we're going to be trapped. Especially if they come in the dark."

"Yes, you're right," I reply and then ask Kuniko and Eve what they found as far as transportation on their scouting trip.

"Nothing before we ran into that pack," Eve answers. "As soon as we saw them, we turned right back here. We'd passed a few cars and trucks, but when we checked them out, there were no keys or the batteries were dead."

This is becoming a common problem now that we're a few years out from the end of the world—cars need attention, too, and it has become more difficult to just hop in an abandoned one and hit the road. Dead batteries, condensation in the gas tanks, or missing keys are all calling for a tow truck, who are as out of business as everyone else.

"Okay. We'll need to get going and look farther, and we should get started now. Let's all go aside from Cody and Bob. Cody can keep watch, and Bob can finish his sculpture," I say with a grin in Bob's direction. "Once we're down on land, we can split up and cover more ground. Eve, you, Kuniko, and Irish can squeeze in the cart, and Morgan and I will take Amy with us on foot. Gear up."

Everyone does, and we head off, both dogs happily trotting alongside Morgan and me. Any time a dog can go for a walk or car ride, he or she is a happy dog. The fact that ours seem to like slaughtering zombies—and, luckily, have a knack for it—is an added bonus.

I feel we'll find something soon as we march back down the bridge, though all the car dealerships are on the Bluffton side of things, which won't help us since they're on the wrong side of the wall. We'll have to find some vehicles, enough to carry all of us easily back and forth between wherever we settle and the wall since that's going to have to be monitored 24/7 for 365 days a year. I would say 366 for the leap years, but no one knows when those are going to be any more. Hell, no one knows what day it is either, or what time, so let's just say they're going to need guards all the time.

We do what we have always done—methodical searches through the houses we come across, one person leading, and the other two providing cover through the building to confirm it's clear of monsters before relaxing and seeing what useful things may be around. Water, canned food, and booze are in plentiful supply while weapons are not.

Amy finds an eye-wateringly bright yellow four-door Jeep Wrangler, its soft top retracted, in one of the garages, and luckily, it has four-wheel drive and is an automatic. The owner had been a thoughtful one. The gas tank is full, and the battery has been pulled and is sitting on a nearby shelf.

It's likely the owners had been snowbirds, and the Jeep was their fun beach vehicle that was left here when they went to their other home. It cranks after only a couple of tries once I hook up the battery.

Transportation, check.

People? None.

Zombies? None.

Some bodies here and there, both kinds, but long dead.

There's something unexplained here; for an island this size with a fairly big population, it doesn't make a lot of sense for there not to be more people (alive, dead, or undead), but regardless, we're pleased to find nothing dangerous and will take a break when we get one.

A few hours pass, and we come across nothing new after the Jeep house, though one sprawling place has a four-car garage with not one but two muscle cars resting inside. A 1969 Mustang fastback, black paint, red interior, fat tires around classic chrome five-spoke wheels, and a four speed smiles at me from a shadowy corner, and we make a date for a later time. There's also a bright-green Road Runner next to it. I know less about the years on those; I have been a Mustang freak my whole life but love all the noisy, fast, so-very-American classics from the late 1960s and early 1970s, and so I'm pleased to see we'll have some toys to sort out. Bob being an engineer is hopefully a good sign since while Ned had been a shade tree mechanic, Ned is dead, baby.

We let Amy drive the Jeep back toward the rest of the group, and it's possible the smile on her face is the biggest I've ever seen. She's been pretty silent since we left New

York, though she's a quiet kid to begin with, but driving sure seems to perk her up. I've been driving for long enough, and making the shitty commute in and out of Charlotte for long enough, to have some of the shine of the pure exhilaration and freedom of being on the road come off. Sure, she wanders off the pavement some as she looks around, and she drives like a grandmother for speed, but frankly, who gives a shit? She'll figure it all out, and we now have our own private racetrack.

Everyone reconvenes as the sun is listing toward the horizon, leaving us only a couple of hours at most until dark, so we're going to spend another night at the wall. Eve's group has come across an indifferent silver sedan that starts, so we are set for getting around as needed. The thought is two people will be on guard at the wall. Some redundancy for staying awake at night since they'll keep each other company, and if trouble comes a-walking, one can jump in a vehicle and come get the rest of us fairly quickly. It'll be about an eight-to-ten-minute drive from the wall to the hotel, and if we get the hot rods rolling, it'll be a bit shorter than that. Bob's porcupine defenses are done, and the outside of the wall bristles with dozens of jagged spears of metal that menace any approach. Anyone trying to scale the wall will be cut to ribbons.

Cody has come up with the idea of setting the claymore mines at alternating intervals on either side of the incoming walls, pointed toward the center, so if triggered by the wires that we'll run up to the top of the wall, anything out on the surface will be hit with a horrifying hail of whirring metal in an unavoidable cross fire. Great idea. That careful installation work will come over the next few days, with a cautious descent via a ladder down to the road's surface. Once we have that in place, and the minigun Bob's going to weld to the top platform of the stairs is finished, it's going to be really, *really* tough for someone (or thing) to come to Hilton Head. I bet the locals wish they thought of this at times back in the past. Like summer.

***

It's another quiet night for the group. On the western coast of Africa, however, a small wind begins to swirl oh-so gently, picking up moisture in bits and pieces and organizing itself loosely in a circular motion. So far, it isn't too interested in being a serious thing, but 'tis the season after all.

# CHAPTER 14

The following morning creeps to life with the reddish-golden gleam of the massive boiling orb of the sun rising gradually over the horizon behind the group to soak the bridge in welcoming light. It's going to be hot and humid again; a weather forecaster here has the easiest job in the world for about six months.

"Well, folks, it's May here in Hilton Head. Let's just get this out of the way all at once, why don't we? It's going to be hot and humid with a good chance of thunderstorms. Every day, all day. See you in late October for a more exciting update when it's hurricane season."

Drops the mike and walks off the set to gather his golf clubs.

\*\*\*

We leave Bob to his next welding project and Cody to begin stringing the mines. Irish remains on the wall for lookout duty, and the rest head into the depths of the island. Hilton Head is organized into what they call "plantations," which seems a smidge dicey in these (or, rather, those) days of sensitivity, but they'd gotten away with it, so there you go. Each of the plantations is usually accessible through one entry/exit road and is eventually guarded by a manned gate for access control. The one we're planning on settling in is roughly in the middle of the island and is called "Palmetto Dunes."

After the winding access road off the main drag, there's a three-way traffic circle, and on the far side looms our new home. The rather drab-looking concrete and glass hotel has been there a long time and is dull to look at, but it's a big building, is going to give us a good line of sight, and may have generators. It certainly will have enough beds to choose from, and balconies ring every floor so if we open all the sliding doors and interior suite doors, we can generate a steady breeze. A pool, too, though we have the Atlantic pool right there beyond the empty sprawl of the beach.

We patrol in armed pairs and go through every floor, every room, and all the exterior spaces and find nothing. No zombies, no people. The hotel isn't undisturbed, not like in a creepy horror movie when everything is exactly the way it ought to be except for the missing residents. No, there are a few dirty glasses and plates and such in the restaurant and a few bunched-up towels tossed indifferently on the outdoor furniture. Other than that, there's not much and nothing that indicates the chaos of a mass invasion and flight or fight. Just a forlorn, empty feeling to the place, which is probably what the whole island felt like in the winter months for the most part.

It makes sense to be off the ground floor for security purposes, and there are no guest rooms there anyway, but the top floor will be something of a pain in the ass to live on since all the elevators are permanently out of order, and I know going up and down ten or so flights of stairs all the time will get old. Maybe Morgan will enjoy it, but the rest of us will not, so we pick the fifth floor as our base as a compromise. It provides a clear view back toward the body of the island above the trees and lets us go up or down if needed in an emergency. I make a mental note to locate a phone book and search for family amusement places nearby, specifically one that may have zip lines we can steal and move here to run from one of the balconies down to the beach.

There's one set of emergency exit stairs on each end of the floor. We secure those by tying their handles with come-along straps to the dormant vending machines located in nearby alcoves. Anyone trying to pull the doors open will have to be strong enough to drag a commercial-grade machine across enough space to gain entry without snapping the door handle off. When we're coming and going, we'll untie one end and retie it when needed so we won't have to stand guard here at the hotel too—just the wall.

Everyone chooses a room and leaves three open for Bob, Cody, and Irish. Eve, Kuniko, and Morgan select adjacent rooms on the ocean side of the hotel, and Amy decides she's going to bunk in with Eve for now but reserves the right to have sleepovers wherever else she chooses. I decide someone ought to be on the boring side with a view of the landward approach, so I take one in the middle of the floor that holds a king-sized bed. The bathrooms are almost a tease—the luxury of a huge shower with paired heads standing useless across from the non-running sink makes me close the door in annoyance since it reminds me that any nocturnal trips to the bathroom means going all the way down to the ground floor and off into the woods. Five floors down. In the dark. I resolve to not drink much water in the later part of the afternoons or maybe talk to Bob about rigging up some, uh, let's say "gutters" that lead to the ground for overnight use in the rooms. But it's a nice room, bright and spacious. And it's across the hall, offset by one room, from Eve's room in case she, too, decides to have a sleepover.

And then we do what we always do. We break into two groups: Morgan, Eve, and Amy go off in one direction, and Kuniko comes with me. We're going to search for zombies, people, food, water, guns, ammo, weed, clothes, other weapons, sunscreen, bathing suits, etc. You name it, we're going to collect it and turn that hotel into an enormous pantry of survival gear.

*I see what you said there in the middle. You said "weed." Planning on sitting on the beach in the twilight with your girl, listening to the waves' endless crash onto the shore, and smoking a fatty? Well, I was going to make fun of you for that,* "dude," *but that actually sounds kind of nice. Carry on.*

It takes a long time to go through houses since one person leads, and one covers, and you never, *ever* let your guard down since those fucking monsters like to wait sometimes and pop out of a closet, just like in a scary movie. Or an upstate New York cabin. We need to keep the discipline up all the time, and it can get old. I'd been in a good job to prepare for this kind of work back in the day, which was largely made up of looking at spreadsheets and data files for hours at a time, so I don't really mind the thoroughness of the task. But there are a lot of damn houses in Palmetto Dunes. It's going to take us a couple of weeks to cover it all, but we'll accumulate a lot of useful stuff along the way.

We've gone through a half dozen in relative silence, Kuniko and I, before she pipes up in her quiet voice, "Do you think we're going to be safe here? I like it that we haven't found any more of them, that seems like a good sign. Kind of weird though too." She says this softly from behind me in one of the dark hallways of a sprawling house, which initially startles me since she's eerily quiet and keeps quite to herself, maybe even more than I do.

I'm content in silence; content in conversation, too, but generally wait for others to start a chat. Kuniko's similar as far as I can tell. We know she'd been through a hard time back at the compound in Kansas, and I guess it was worse at times, more so than she's shared with anyone. She still dresses modestly, even in the heat here, and keeps the dark sheet of her hair down most of the time, obscuring her delicate, pretty features. While Kuniko got more comfortable over time with our group in New York, the addition of Irish and, probably to a greater extent, Cody, has set her back to old habits.

"I hope so," I answer. "I feel like a politician when I say it like that, but we know there are no guarantees. So far, so good though, right? Well, aside from that batch that came after us, but they tend to herd together a bit, so maybe that was all of them. It'd be nice to be that lucky."

"That's true. I want it to be. It feels like we're going to be safe, finally. It's pretty here too. Not the same kind of pretty as your family's place, but it's also peaceful without other people crowding things. I'm happy we are here, even though …" She trails off and doesn't continue.

I wait a moment or two to see if she'll finish the thought, trying to guess what it is. We keep moving through the house and come back to the front door. Nothing has been unique here, just a couple of flats of water we've set on the front porch for pickup later. No weapons unless we plan on using garden tools, and if it all comes to that, we're going to be in deeper shit than we've ever been, so we just leave those in the garage. Instead of moving immediately to the next house, I sit on the brick stairs leading back to ground level—every house here has the living quarters a story off the ground in case of nasty storms—to see if I can subtly coax whatever is troubling her out into the open. I pull one of the waters out of the shrink-wrap and offer it up to her and then take another for myself.

She hesitates, opening the bottle and drinking a sip before sitting beside me, still silent at first. "You're good, you know that? I see what you did, so simple and gentle about letting me decide to talk if I wanted to, without pressing me. Eve is lucky. We're all lucky actually."

I'm embarrassed by this, but there's nothing to say. Eve and I are still in some kind of in-between place where we gravitate toward one another, and speaking for myself, I crave her company, still watching her from the corner of my eye whenever given the chance. She'll come in often to sleep with me—sometimes facing me, but most times facing away but tucked against me—but we've kept the last step, I don't know, on hold. I'm going to let her lead us there, but there are days when it's hard to wait for her. I want her miserably but in a happy sort of way, if that's possible.

Kuniko breaks into my thoughts. "Cody makes me uncertain. Not that I think he is dangerous exactly, but in a reckless way perhaps."

"You mean when he kissed you after the fight? I saw that and saw the look on your face. I can have a talk with him if you want me to."

"No. I didn't want him to do that, but I was surprised more than anything else. We'd all just been killing them but from a distance, and then you and Morgan left us to go and, well, execute the remaining ones. In a way, that was upsetting to me—both the leaving us to take that chance and how good you are at it. I've seen you fight before, both of you, and it can be frightening in more than one way. That never occurred to me until that very moment. We wouldn't all survive without you two, so to watch you risk everyone's safety, in a sense, was concerning. And the joy that Morgan takes in it … well, that's a thing you never saw in the old days. You look like you are concentrating and doing a job almost, but she smiles while she is killing. It's terrifying to watch, while comforting at the same time since she's one of us. Anyway, that jumble of thoughts was in my head, then the relief that they were all dead, but none of those were happy places exactly, so when he kissed me, it just didn't seem to fit the moment. I just rambled a lot, but does it all make sense?"

It does, and I have never looked at things in that manner before, so I need a minute to kick it around in my head. "Cody is a boy though, a young boy, and I think he was just excited by the moment. I don't think he meant anything more than that, like in the past, in that place …. But he *is* impulsive, and we have to watch him. I worry he is going to leap before looking at the wrong time."

I think it's funny we aren't much more than a handful-plus-a-couple-more-years older than Cody and are talking about him like he's an early teen, but I understand. He put his rifle to the back of my neck when he should have been shooting the bad guys; that had been out of fear and was misdirected toward me since I was the one waiting on Ajax, so I see where she's going.

"Okay," I say. "Good points, all of them. We'll make sure that whoever is paired up with him is a balancing influence. Are you all right with being on guard at the same time as him out at the wall? I haven't sat down and figured out a rotation, but I can keep you apart if you need me to."

"No. Maybe I will be good for him, as you said, a balance. I just needed to get all this out of my head and for you to hear. You need to know that we need you, and Morgan, to stay alive."

I see what she does there too.

***

While we never count the days exactly since there isn't much point, we gather and patrol for what may be a couple of weeks before being satisfied with the idea that we're alone on the island, as surprising and weird as that is. We haven't been able to cover the entire island, not yet, but have patrolled out for a mile or more in every direction. We begin to unwind a little, where the paired guards at the wall are the only ones actively "working" once we've largely unloaded the mammoth grocery store across the main road from the plantation. The shelves and stockroom contain an absolute bounty of everything we need, and grills and cooking items are plentiful there and within the hotel. Grills now sit on several of the unused balconies for cooking the soup and other canned items we use as our staples, but Irish has also accumulated some fishing gear and supplemented the expiring food with whatever fresh catch she brings each day.

It's quiet. We're at the beach, and it seems we're alone and safe. It's awesome. We take long walks on the beach, collecting shells like any dorky set of tourists. Well, tourists who carry guns all the time, but everyone greatly enjoys the new location and we settle into ordinary routines for the first time in years.

Morgan is typical restless Morgan, however, and volunteers for guard duty more than her fair share and insists on running from the hotel to the wall, letting whoever she's paired with drive there. I think she's hoping something will happen to give her an outlet for the furious energy that can't be contained. When off duty, she'll take bicycle rides all over the island, claiming she's still unsatisfied that we're safe. Others will join her from time to time, though will return after a while, sweaty and frustrated by Morgan's relentless drive. Sadly, for some of us, that gives her an idea: training.

All kinds of training. Running, both long distances and sprints. Bike rides, strength training in the giant gym in the hotel, swimming in the ocean—"If we get in trouble," she insists, "we can swim back to the mainland if we have to"; fat chance of that, though, since it's far, and the inland waterway is strongly tidal—hand-to-hand combat, whatever she comes up with for the day. I'm used to this, as are Eve and Amy from our earlier time in New York, but Kuniko, Bob, Irish, and Cody all suffer at first. Morgan is more capable than the soldiers are at the interpersonal fighting, which Morgan likes to remind Cody about from their first meeting, and she drives them harder than everyone else as a result. In fact, she pushes Cody harder on everything.

He hates it at first, and maybe hates her too. He'd come back from the sessions red faced, dripping with sweat, and angry from the never-ending prodding. It takes a while for them to run into it (ha, ha), but he finally finds something he's better at than her: sprinting. He's a stupid-fast kid over fairly short distances.

I'm fast, Morgan is faster, and today, we find out that Cody is a rock star.

It's a shift change for watch, with Morgan and Amy coming off, but they arrive early, a little before Eve and I are due at the wall. We don't have working watches anymore but have found windup kitchen timers that function just fine to keep track of the hours. Morgan says Amy has been complaining about the training and wants a day off. In typical fashion, she decides we're going to have to earn it, and if we fail to do so, she may take things up a level.

Morgan sets markers on the beach, perhaps 150 yards away down on the hard-packed sand close to the outgoing tide, and tells us all if someone beats her, we can all have the next day off. She even offers to race us sequentially so she'll become more tired as we go through the group.

Bob is smart, though, and huddles us off to the side for some strategizing. "Let me go first, then Amy. You all know how Morgan is. She's going to run close to full speed for all of them because she's not someone who wins by a little bit. With my cut Achilles, and Amy's shorter legs, no offense, we can burn a little bit of her steam off." He points around the group to Irish, Kuniko, Eve, and then me. "You four go next. I know she'll work hardest to beat you," he says when looking at me. "And then Cody. I've seen you run some in the distance torture. I think you're leaving something in the tank, aren't you?"

Cody nods enthusiastically. "Yeah, I ran track in high school, short-distance stuff. We had to run cross-country, too, but I was way better at drag races. The army kept us running all the time too. You know that. Run somewhere, carry a ton of shit, shoot some guns, stand around a lot, eat, repeat. I'm going to run that bitch into the sand. Sorry," he says with an apologetic glance in my direction.

"It's okay. I want to beat her too. You all have just met her, but she has been pushing me my whole life. I swear, she'd poke me in the ass with a fork when I was a baby learning to crawl just to get me moving faster."

That brings a chuckle of laughter and lightens the mood a little. We agree that each of us will run as hard as we can to do whatever we can to wear her down, and then walk back to meet her.

"Ready? Got yourselves a little plan? Let's do this," Morgan says with a toss of her hair before she ties it back into a ponytail. The other women do the same, with serious looks of concentration all around.

Everyone's in bathing suits—it's hot and muggy all the time, and we wear as little as possible. Sunscreen is a daily routine, and there's already a trash can on the patio by the pool full of the empty spray cans. I'm both pleased and bothered that Eve is wearing the yellow bikini from before, which barely covers her figure and is a tiny bit transparent. It's distracting, and I'm glad she'll be running away from me—I can't stop surreptitiously looking at her all the time anyway, and that swimsuit is torture. Everyone is in great shape, even Bob as our elder statesman. A forced diet and Morgan's daily boot camp of hell will do that for you, and I suppose an observer would be impressed with the fitness of the group.

Off we go.

Bob is game—while his injured foot limits his speed, he's a grinder when we're all running. There's no quit in him. He has a gritty stubbornness I admire since he isn't going to win anything we're challenged to accomplish by the Wicked Witch of the Beach, but he never, *ever* gives up. Aside from me, no one else can say that. I'll drag myself down the sand if I have to before surrendering, but I have a lifetime of practice with Morgan. I love my sister dearly, but she's a handful. All the time.

Morgan smokes Bob, Amy, Eve, Irish, and Kuniko without much effort. She's a rare athlete, a world-class one who does anything she sets her mind and body to, easily picking up every sport and becoming an expert quickly. When you watch her move, it's so naturally effortless for her, it takes you a moment to recognize the fact that she's running faster, jumping higher, throwing farther, and whatever else better than everyone and making it look easy.

I make her work for it. By the time she's run the first five, she's breathing a little heavily since whoever is up next has scooted to the starting line as soon as the prior race is done in order to shorten her break.

"Ready, little brother? Wanna race?" she says with the usual grin at the usual jibe.

"Ready to lose? I'm fresher than you are. My turn this time."

"Not happening today, junior. Enjoy eating my sand."

"Big talk. I should've told you this before now, but you run like a girl."

She cups her hands under both boobs and gives them a little wiggle, drawing a guffaw from Bob and a gasp from Amy. "In case you've missed it over the years, I *am* a girl. You, my least favorite brother, need to now get ready to *lose* to a girl."

She beats me, but only by a single step—we're right next to each other at the end. I get out to a quicker start, but she reels me in and barely passes me in the last handful of steps. I acknowledge she's won but then jog back to the start, forcing her to burn a tiny bit more energy.

Cody is alert enough to be waiting, stretched, and is ready to go.

"Army boy goes last. Good. This was fun, but you're all going to be working your asses off tomorrow. Long run, weights, *and* a swim coming at you."

I hear Eve groan in the background. Cody doesn't say anything, just sets his mouth firmly and stares down at the markers by the finish line.

"Cat got your tongue, kid?"

"The name's Cody. You could try that out sometime. But what you're going to call me is 'winner' in about fifteen seconds. Now, shut your mouth and run."

Amy steps between them, getting ready to count them down, and looks at Cody with a pleading look. Morgan stares at him for a second, annoyed, and, I note with some pride, a little redder in the face and sweatier than before our race. She turns to the "track" and nods at Amy.

"Go!"

They tear off barefoot down the sand, kicking it up behind them as they dig for maximum speed and traction off the line. Cody is out front immediately, but while I know Morgan could close well, he never gives up the lead. Running in sand is never a graceful thing, but Cody looks like he's hovering over it, barely touching down. I watch

Morgan strain with all her God-given ability and iron will, but she has no chance. He flickers across the finish at least four or five steps ahead of her and says something briefly to her when she slows to a stop. She looks as if she's going to reply but then closes her mouth. Cody then trots back to us with a huge smile on his face.

"Vacation day tomorrow, people," he says as he high-fives and fist-bumps his way through all of us on his way down to the cooling waves.

The rest of the group follow him while I wait for my sister. She walks back with a sullen expression on her face, stopping next to me.

"What did he say to you?"

She's angry, I know that. My sister stares at me for a moment, then off at the frolicking bunch down at the waterfront, including the dogs. "He said he could go faster."

Ah. Not only did she lose, and maybe get outwitted a smidge in the process, and get a little smack talk at the end, but she has a new obsession. There's nothing on earth that will prevent her from trying to beat him, and as soon as possible. I pity Cody since he'll be running up and down this stretch until his feet bleed, or out on the myriad bike paths that are everywhere. I pity her a tiny bit too—the drive that makes her awesome also makes her unhappy at times.

I hug her to me, not saying anything, and the two of us stand in the strong breeze watching our friends celebrate. Then I remember how she'd been about to say something back to Cody before she stopped herself. "What *didn't* you say to him?"

Morgan looks at me again, this time less angrily since she's cooling off, and then smiles the smile she's reserved only for me for decades. The one that lights her face and brings the beauty out from under the sweat and sand. The one that says she has a secret and will only share it with her brother and no one else. "That I could go faster too. You guys needed the day off."

Well, what do you know. "I'm proud of you," I say, hugging her from the side.

"Yeah, whatever. If you tell anyone, I'm going to punch you in the nuts."

\*\*\*

Eve and I drive the Jeep out to the wall, conscious it has been unmanned for over an hour, and I don't realize at first that I'm driving ever more slowly as we get close to the bridge. My subconscious may have put me on guard, and I find myself scanning the periphery out of old habit, which are now new habits that will never die unless *I'm* planning on dying. Rough new world with this mix of living in a semi-tropical paradise with a good group of people but always watching for it to be torn away from us.

But we see nothing on the way and park the four-wheeler facing back toward our new home once we arrive, just in case—more new habits. Nothing visible out over the wall and to the horizon either; just the mammoth glowing orb of the setting sun burning the edge of the world as it surrenders the day. Full dark will be some time coming. It's a beautiful sight now, with the fading light painting the waves a happy golden orange as they walk their way out to the ocean. It feels ... well, normal.

Eve is quiet by nature, as am I. I have always been comfortable with silence and used that effectively over time since most people are not and will typically fill it after a few moments, saying something they don't really mean to. I've been something of a loner all my life, so I don't mind my own company nor the quiet that comes with it. Here we are, sitting and watching the world, which ticks along, ignoring the fact there are a lot less people wandering around its surface and consuming everything they can as selfishly as possible. The world doesn't give a shit and goes on doing all of its usual things; the things fewer people appreciated of late. Too much heads down at tiny phone screens, skipping the simple and wonderful things all around them.

*Easy up there on the soapbox. You got to choose what you wanted to do, so did all of them. Granted, they were a consumptive, entitled bunch, but you also have to admit there were plenty of good eggs in the basket too. Just easier to remember the one asshole who cut you off on the drive to work and to underappreciate the woman you saw who took her jacket off when it began to rain and gave it to the homeless man lying by the side of the road, or the security guard who triggered the automatic door for you every morning. Not that you needed it, but she probably did it because you also said "good morning" to her and chatted for a second every day while others whizzed by, as if she was a piece of furniture. Yeah, the asshole ratio out of each hundred people was maybe climbing, but that's kind of sorted itself out, hasn't it?*

True, all of that.

I relax and just listen to the wind, the gulls calling, and the nothing. The two of us sit on the stairs, both on the same side and just look out, not talking, not touching.

After a while, Eve startles me out of my thoughts. "I've been waiting, you know."

She changed out of the wet yellow bathing suit after the celebration in the water and is wearing a baggy University of Georgia hooded sweatshirt and tan cotton cargo shorts. Her hair is pulled back away from her face, and she looks like she always does, very pretty and delicate, almost fragile. The toughness is there too—it's for all of us, but there's still that something that makes you want to take her in your arms and protect her from the world. The receding sun's rays bring out tiny gold flecks in her brown eyes and turn her tanned skin a honey hue, like the waves marching inexorably far below us. I can't get enough of looking at her.

"Waiting for what?"

"Us."

She doesn't say anything else for a moment, and I leave it unfilled, just watch the light play across her fine features. I know she'll say something when she has something to say, not just to say something.

"I know I told you this once, but it feels like a very long time ago. I still like it when you look at me like that. It makes me feel good and normal in the middle of ..." she pauses and waves an arm out over in the direction of the mainland, "all of this."

She breathes in and continues. "I told you this too. I need you. We all need you. To hold us together and tell us what to do. To watch over us no matter what is happening. To find us places like this, where maybe we can be safe. To settle people down, especially when Morgan does Morgan things. She needs you more than everyone else does, except me. You were the first person I saw after it all ended," she says with another wave. "You kept me safe, you let me just be there in the house with you without asking anything in return. And Jack. You kept him away, and the zombies too. I'm not cut out for this kind of world, the violence and need for action, and killing when you have to. You know that, and you protect me. All this time, we've been together, and you even let me do what I needed to do with my father. You did the hardest thing to do with people you care for: let them go."

All those memories come flooding back.

When the first alpha zombie we'd met dropped Eve off at my minifortress back in North Carolina, and she was furious with me for making her strip so I could confirm she wasn't bitten—funny how the first day, hell, the first fifteen minutes, I met her, I saw her naked but haven't since; things don't usually work out in that sequence. When she first came into my room for a sleepover after realizing I wanted nothing from her. Then our drive to New York, where we stopped at the house her parents lived in to see if they'd survived—her father had but was dying. When I left her behind at her insistence, despite my fears and misgivings, and continued on the trip with DeeDee and Amelie. When she later arrived on the same day as Morgan, bringing Amy and Ned with her from the winter in Pennsylvania. Her telling me she needed me for the first time while we sat on the porch, waiting to see if the next thing she was going to do was shoot me in the face after I'd been bitten by a zombie. All those memories.

My mother told me something very wise once, back when I was in my early twenties. Mothers do that more often than we all admit, but this one took a while to finally hit home. I had been in a few long relationships in a row, none of which ended up working out, and was beginning to think that since I was the only repeated part of the equation, perhaps I needed to look more closely in the mirror.

My mom and I were sitting in the kitchen one morning. I lived with my folks at that time, trying to save money to get my own place. Nothing special about the morning, just me drinking coffee and her drinking some pretend tea. I say "pretend" because she mostly just waved a tea bag over hot water and called it done. I'd been telling her how the latest girlfriend wasn't working out, and how it seemed like I might be the problem.

"You're just going to know when you've found the one," she said, looking at me and then back to her magazine. "You'll know."

And that was it. Sometimes, you hear something smart, and it doesn't come back around as being so until later.

Eve jumps over my thoughts again. "I'm waiting for us because I don't want to be looking over my shoulder all the time, afraid that it'll be ripped away. I couldn't bear that. I can handle waiting. I think it's better to want something and not have it than it is to get it and lose it.

"I want us to be safe. I want to be with you and not in-between like a couple of high school kids too shy to speak to each other. I want you, all of you."

I keep looking at her as she says all of this, feeling a bit of an anxious flutter in my chest, the one that's always there when I'm close to Eve but now stronger than usual.

She takes my hand between hers and looks back at me in that direct, inquisitive way she has. "Say something?"

What I want to say is "I know," but that won't make any sense to her. "Thank you for telling me all of that. We're going to be safe. Somehow, we're going to. I don't care what it takes. And then we're going to … I want to walk on the beach and hold hands with you when we're old. And …"

"And what?"

My mind is running ahead to a future where we just live. No running, no hiding, no fighting. A simpler version where we all just figure it out and keep things uncomplicated in the world. A world with small people in it, too, who'll get a better chance.

"Still there?" she asks again, watching me steadily.

"And, you know, kids," I answer finally, looking away at the horizon, a little embarrassed for saying it out loud.

Eve reaches over and gently turns my face back to hers, smiling just as gently but with a hint of a mischievous gleam in her eyes. "You know we'd have to sleep together to have children."

"I've heard rumors that that was needed."

The bit of a twinkle in her eye for some insane reason makes me think of Santa Claus. Like when Santa is thinking about giving Mrs. Claus a proper rogering, I suppose.

*Moron. Stay on topic. Santa Claus? Now? What is* wrong *with you?*

"I'm still not sure I can actually have children, remember?"

I'm mortified to say this, sure that the red blush rampaging across my face rivals the setting sun, but can't stop myself. "I guess we'll have to practice a lot to be sure."

She smiles a little wickedly at me and squeezes my hand, letting her gaze linger on my face before looking out over the water and marshland. What else is there to say after all that? I want to kiss her so badly, I can practically taste her lips, but I know that 1) it'll ruin the moment, and 2) it won't stop at that. She's right, we need to wait until we're safe. And it's good to want things.

We sit in comfortable silence again and watch the sun go down. On our wall, hoping we're safe from a world full of monsters. How will we know when it's safe? When it's over?

*Hey, let me know when we're heading down to the water for a cold bath!*

No kidding.

# CHAPTER 15

We do have a busier time than the typical people who used to visit the island. Much more work than play as we try to accumulate as much as we can and prepare for the chance of an invasion. It bothers me that aside from the group we'd wiped out, we haven't seen any more zombies. "Bothered me" is a misnomer since no one in their right mind should be troubled by the absence of killing machines, but it feels like a nagging unanswered question. Maybe it's a question that's never going to get answered, not like we can ask anyone, but this island holds tens of thousands of year-round residents. That's a tempting and relatively captive food supply for zombies. Which begs the question: Where are the people? We've found a few bodies in our searches, hidden in rooms in some of the houses, just dead in bed or with their arms wrapped around children, or out in the open with a few zombie corpses scattered nearby. But not a lot.

Over the course of time, we have searched, cleared, and taken useful items from every house, condo, and hotel room within Palmetto Dunes and the adjacent plantations, which is no small task. Clothes, a small cache of weapons—though mostly pocketknives and a handful of handguns—food and water, a ton of DVDs and battery-powered travel players for those, and anything else you can imagine. The movies are a welcome respite from reality, just like they were in the past, though we all avoid the horror genre—those find their way into a discard pile. Thank you but no. We have any and all of that we need. The rest of our collection runs the gamut from animated, G-rated stuff to what-the-hell-are-those-people-doing X-rated films, which also are largely ignored—though, I wonder about Cody. We also come across an amazing assortment of prescription and non-prescription drugs, including plenty of pot and assorted powders and pills we dump out.

Our floor turns into an oversized version of my house back in North Carolina. Rooms for canned food, all organized by expiration date and type—canned veggies over there in aisle three, soups in row two. Several rooms for bottled water since we now have no fresh water supply like we did at the lake—not that we ever drank the lake water, of course, since that's full of fish poo, but rather drew it from the spring—an armory, and then a room for everything else, like towels, sunscreen, and so on. I have always had the mindset to enjoy what the planet gives me, whether it's a view, a scent, or its resources, wanting to immerse myself in those gifts without spoiling them for anyone else. An old-fashioned paradigm in current times, but it lets me sleep well at night. As a result, it troubles me from time to time that we have to dispose of things without washing or reusing them as often as I would like, but we don't have access to washing machines for clothes or dishware, and so we do the best we can to minimize our waste. The nice thing is we do so on an unspoken basis.

It isn't all work, though, and Morgan even gives or makes us earn periodic breaks from the torturous exercise regimen she's imposed. We enjoy the beach and ocean, play Frisbee or toss a football, nap, build astonishing sandcastles—Bob is phenomenal, as is Kuniko with her creative nature—and do the things visitors have always done on beach vacations. There's even a day where we bring cases and cases of beer bottles out to the wall, as many as will fit in the vehicles, and hoist them onto the platforms. Rather than getting drunk, we all throw the bottles as far out beyond the barrier as we can to create yet another barricade—a jagged carpet of shattered glass from side to side, fifty yards deep from the foot of our barricade and several inches thick. It's fun and noisy and ultimately smelly, but practical. Broken glass won't stop an attack but will certainly accomplish two things: 1) an early alert if something comes in the night since anyone stepping on it will make a racket, and 2) while zombies don't seem to feel pain, a foot full of embedded shards of glass will slow them down a little at least.

We also settle into a pattern of patrols, mostly in the Jeep, though Morgan insists on foot patrol several times a week, leading a bedraggled assortment of us on runs in the direction of the day. It's worse than the (so far lucky) tedium of sitting at the wall and trying to maintain focus. As for the southern side of the island, we've mostly left it alone to date—it's several miles away from us, and we simply haven't gotten there yet. We agree it's important to check it out soon since we have the unsolved mystery of missing neighbors, and so we find a map and draw out patterns to take in order to whittle down the sections of the island we need to search through and clear.

Today is the day for the southern end. I'm on patrol in the Jeep, Irish riding shotgun beside me, quite literally since that's what she's carrying. We leave the soft top down permanently—no point in limiting our line of sight or fire. While it rains seemingly every day here, we frankly don't care if the Jeep gets a little soggy—it's a Jeep, after all, and is made to handle stuff like that, though we usually keep it parked under the porte cochere when not in use. This afternoon, we're granted a clear day with fairly low humidity and a steady breeze coming from the east, maybe a little stronger than an ordinary day, but whenever storms roll in here, they can either bring or push a lot of air with them, so we take no immediate note of it.

I had been to Hilton Head only once before, with four other guys on a poorly organized and executed attempt at a bachelor party weekend. While this is a fun place, especially for families with small kids, it turns out it's not exactly a hotspot for twentysomething mischief makers intent on seeing naked boobies. The Friday of that weekend, we got drunk enough at some of the clustered restaurants and bars, but after asking around for "those" kinds of establishments, we ended up disappointed to find out they simply weren't here. Rather than move the party somewhere else, we grudgingly agreed to stick with golf on Saturday and Sunday and just see if we could find a group of like-minded single girls on Saturday night to get into a little trouble together. None of the guys were close friends of mine—I honestly had very few of those—but they were coworkers, and the bachelor was a good-enough guy, so I'd agreed to come along.

On Saturday afternoon, I went out for a run, while the others were napping off the golf beer—which I had skipped; golf was tough enough sober—since I liked to explore places on foot whenever I could to get a real feel for the area. Three miles or so into the run, I had been considering turning around since you always had to go all the way back, too, and I was not going to walk it in the burning July heat. Running in the hot weather wasn't pleasant either, but you created your own small breeze and got it over with more quickly and would be fine if you drank enough water. At least, I told myself that—running wasn't fun for me, but it was a helluva good way to sweat.

I had come to one of the multiple-lane traffic circles that dotted the island, confusing the shit out of tourists (maybe on purpose) and aggravating the locals who knew what they were doing, and I spotted a guard house on the far side a few hundred yards down the road. That seemed like a logical landmark to reverse course, so I played a careful game of Frogger and hopped across the traffic, exited the far side of the circle, and reached the gate welcoming me to Sea Pines. Except it wasn't actually welcoming; you had to pay a few bucks to visit by car or show a resident's pass. That seemed stupid. All the touristy sections of the island were nice, most of them were access controlled, but apparently, someone decided that section was even nicer and managed to get away with putting up a barrier and charging for access. I watched a few people fall for it, a little disgusted at the idea.

*Everyone's free to do what they want, remember, even if it's stupid. Just because it doesn't make sense to you, Captain Logical, doesn't make it wrong. Wasteful and silly, sure, but if the sheep want to fall for it, who are you to care? It's their time and money after all.*

Stubbornness runs in a strong streak through my family. While Morgan's outrageous behavior in our youth had allowed me to get away with lesser offenses, if pressed, my parents would have said I have my own issue with authority. It's more about challenging it than disrespecting it; I have been brought up properly to respect others, but intangible, invisible authority pushes my buttons sometimes, and I push back. That has stuck with me throughout my lifetime, but at least over time, I've acknowledged it as something for me to be mindful of, whether I choose to ignore the warning light or not.

That day in Hilton Head had been one of those times— "someone" had decided everything within the gated area was better than everything without, including the people, which "justified" an entry fee. Which justified me to be a little bit of a dick, even if for my own amusement, sanity, and peace of mind.

*That was a close call. You said "little bit of a dick," which could have come out differently and all kinds of wrong, amigo.*

And the voice inside never, *ever* helps.

At first, I'd decided to stick with the plan and head back, but then out of that stubborn, push-the-rules characteristic, I changed my mind and went for a defiant jog right past the guardhouse and gate, waiting for someone to come out and chase me, fully prepared to make them work for it. No one had, of course, and my run took me deep into the resort. A little disappointed there hadn't been any kind of confrontation, and I knew I'd be walking back since I was now at least six miles away, but I wanted to see it all. Not much of a win exactly, but I was in, and for free, so there.

At the very end of the main road, I'd come to a tourist collection zone, complete with a classic lighthouse, ice cream shops, restaurants, retail shops full of clothes people would never wear at home but happily collected, and a little outdoor stage where apparently some guy came to play guitar for kids on Saturday nights in the summer. It was an utter madhouse full of people running this way and that, chasing kids who were carrying teetering ice cream cones and drizzling snot out of their noses, while trying not to spill their plastic cups of wine—the parents' wine, not the kids—and all of them must have been having a good time since there was a lot of smiling and laughter. To me, it looked and sounded like unbridled chaos when I was seeking solace, and I retreated immediately, overwhelmed by it all. My life had been simple and, admittedly, solitary in general, and my image of a beach vacation was all about peace and near silence. This was mayhem, and I had trouble understanding how all these people were enjoying it. So much for "better"—I was extra happy to have avoided the cover charge. I reversed course, feeling pleased in a juvenile way since I'd beaten the system, but I was also confused by the difference between how I looked at things compared to that horde of people. Maybe if I had children and a family, I'd get it, but it seemed rather nuts.

Irish and I come to that selfsame guardhouse, and all this comes back to me in a flood. Memories are funny like that—they jump out at you in surprising detail, even when it's something or a time you think you've largely forgotten. Not déjà vu, just the brain needing a spark to connect past to present.

The guardhouse is unmanned, and I'm disappointed in a way that the arm of the gate is up since the rebellious part of me kind of wants to see how tough the gate may actually be when compared to four thousand pounds of Jeep, but I suppress my disappointment.

I let the Wrangler idle for a moment while I noodle around in my thoughts until Irish nudges me with her elbow. "Hey, you gonna drive or not?"

"Whoops," I answer, startled a bit, but getting back into the moment. "My bad. I've been here before and was thinking ahead to what we might find down the road. You know how you can get lost in a memory that comes back deeper than you thought, right?"

I turn to look at her as I say this and notice she looks uneasy, gnawing at her lip. Her Caribbean-descent skin has darkened a little with the added sun exposure over the past weeks, making those green eyes even more riveting. She's pretty, with a broad, open face and easy smile that makes you happy. High, strong cheekbones under a frizzy light-brown mop of hair she struggles to control, though has insisted on letting it grow out now that she's "out of the army." Like all of us, except for Kuniko, she wears as little as possible since the air-conditioning is permanently out, so a dark-brown bikini top mostly covers her, and she wears matching running shorts since running is basically a hobby for all of us thanks to Morgan. We could have run the air-conditioning in the cars, but to me, that feels like longing for the old days versus accepting the new world as it is, warts and all.

Irish is easy to like and is a gritty worker; there have been plenty of days when Cody, Amy, and others have mailed it in on some of the chores while she would keep up with me and Morgan, sweating miserably but uncomplaining. We get along well whenever we're on guard or gathering or patrolling. She'd told us all one night around a bonfire on the beach that she had been a military kid and moved everywhere throughout her youth, seeing nearly all the countries where the US had a presence, and the decision to join when she was old enough was a simple one. However, later learning all the details of what had happened with the colonel and his buddies not just letting the genie out of the bottle but creating it, she'd been disaffected and was happy to be with us. That goes both ways since she's calm and cool under fire, and if, or probably when, we get in another fight, she'll be good to have on our side.

"You okay?" I ask as I resume driving.

She nods sort of sideways, so in no particular direction. "Can I ask you something?"

"Sure. What's up?" I ask, not knowing this will be another case of male equals completely unintuitive. Or maybe it's just me being not intuitive when it comes to girls. I'm good at keeping my head on a swivel when it comes to the zombies, but women keep surprising me.

"So …" she starts and then pauses. I play the wait-and-listen game. "Not sure the best way about this, but remember way back to what I told you all what Cody said to me when we were trapped in the personnel carrier?"

Irish isn't looking at me, just out and around, as is everyone's habit as we pass the gate and enter the resort area surrounded by the sprawling green hillocks and natural areas decorating either side of the road.

"That you were probably going to die in there?"

"That was one of the things he said. But, the other thing. D'you remember? It would be easier if you did. On me."

I think back to when we rescued them and then ran away from the terrifying and sudden attacking wave of thousands of zombies—who were fast … don't forget *fast*—pouring across the fields and stopping for Ajax, and Cody putting his gun on me. After we'd escaped, and I confronted Cody, Irish brought our fisticuffs to a halt and then told us Cody had said … I think he'd said he wanted to have sex before they died. Was that it? I'm not certain—it feels like there's something else there, but it's like trying to catch a soap bubble in the breeze on the beach.

"The thing about having sex?"

"Close enough," she says with a sigh. "This'll take forever if I don't just get it out there. He said he'd never seen a Black girl naked, and he also said the thing about having sex, so yeah. Before we died. Even though we had supplies for a handful of days."

"Okay, yeah, I remember that now. Did he say something to you about that again?" I recall the recent conversation with Kuniko. "Want me to say something to him?"

"No, that's not it! Jesus," she replies, clearly frustrated.

Now I'm lost.

She explains. "Have *you* ever seen a Black girl naked?"

Oh. Uh-oh. I keep driving, now nearing the tourist trap zone by the lighthouse, which is a meandering, picturesque road, so I have to watch where I'm going. I have a tendency— maybe "compulsion" is a better word—to tell the truth, even when perhaps I shouldn't. I was like that even before. In the now, I always feel like if we have secrets from one another, it will cause dissent and distrust within our group, and we rely so heavily on the continued existence of the group that bruised feelings will be an acceptable trade-off for dead humans, so honesty is the best policy. At least, I have (finally) figured out that isn't the real question.

"Irish, ah, um, so ... Eve and I are—"

She interrupts me, a little angrily, which is probably deserved since I'm not exactly getting my thoughts organized well as I try to be diplomatic. "You an' Eve aren't doing shit, and we all know it. You just look at her, and she looks back, but that's it. Excuse my military mouth, but the way I see it, the two of you ought to be humpin' away the day whenever you can, and you ain't. Does she not like you? Is she into girls? Are you? Because there's one sitting right here looking for some comp'ny, bored out of her head with being on guard and waiting and collecting stuff and watching a good-looking, nice man just waiting for whatever it is you're waiting for, thinking we could be having some fun. I'm not looking for marriage, just some affection and to feel good for a while in the middle of all of this shit. What's the harm in any of that? Not like anyone would know. So I'm going to ask you a little different. Do you *want* to see a Black girl naked?"

There's a challenge in her voice that cautions me to think first, think second, and then answer. Holy shit. Holy shit. *Holy shit.*

How to answer … I rack my brain.

If I'd been off-balance a couple of seconds ago, I'm completely thrown now. She may as well have tossed me blindfolded into one of the large roaring breakers coming in when the tide changed and let me sort things out. Irish is pretty, I'm fascinated by Eve, Irish is bored and horny, we're a tiny group that needs to stay closely knit, and she's just asked if we ought to duck off into the bushes and let off a little steam—and maybe some other stuff too—and everything she's said is pretty darn accurate. And even without the voice inside telling me, waiting can be difficult at times, and affection is in short supply these days. I'm not going off for a romp in the bushes with her, but she makes some good logical points, and I don't want to upset her any further. It takes a lot of guts to say what she's just said to me.

I take my eyes off the road this time and face her, road markings be damned—the landscapers can take it up with my butler. I only need to glance now anyway since we're coming up on the huge parking lot at the end of the road. Irish stares back at me, lovely and defiant, green eyes sparking and daring me to say something stupid that will risk blowing everything here to bits. She'll "understand" and "be fine," but she'll stew just as anyone would. Resentment will creep in, toward me, toward Eve, toward all of it. Our little sandy paradise will become toxic, like it had with Jack and Ned in the past, and I can't go through that again.

I let the Jeep coast to a stop and turn to her. "Thank you, and I'm sorry. Those aren't the best words, but they're how I feel," I say and reach across to hug her, me facing toward the rear of the vehicle. She stiffens, which I expected, and I go to say something else. "Any other—"

"What the fuck is that?"

Huh? It's a hug and the beginning of an apology while extending a cautious olive branch, I guess? I try again. "Irish, I know you're upset, but I'm trying to tell you—"

"No, shut up about that. What. Is. *That?* Look!" She thrusts a finger out over my shoulder, toward the lighthouse area.

I pull away from her, glad for a distraction from the awkward moment, and turn around to look through the windshield. And I'm immediately sorry I do.

We've found all of the people. Like the saying went, sometimes you have to be careful for what you wish because when you get it, you're sorry. So very sorry.

The parking lot in the center of the shops, lighthouse, and picnic areas is large enough to hold hundreds of cars, with adjacent grassy sections trampled flat by impatient (or lazy) visitors who had chosen not to hunt for a farther spot, adding another several hundred square yards of open space. The average car can hold four people, and if you're fitting bodies in the same space as a car, you can likely squeeze six or seven people in a vehicle's footprint. If the bodies are stacked on top of one another, the capacity extrapolates in horrible fashion.

We get out without even thinking to turn off the Jeep or put it in neutral, and I barely notice it rolling away from me to come to a crunching rest against a lamppost. This is the most appalling thing I have ever seen, even compared to the early days. Instead of a gathering place of happiness and chaos, it's a charnel house. Human corpses litter the parking lots, draped and broken across picnic tables, huddled in piles underneath the magnificent sprawling trees that shade a small stage. Many are piled atop one another in grotesque pyramids, staring, accusing eyes peering at us. They're uncountable in their silent misery, but at a guess, I put their numbers in the thousands and all shapes, sizes, and ages. A mammoth ebony swath of them to the left are blackened, as if by fire, and I look away quickly before capturing too much detail in the camera eye of my mind. I'm numb, unable to speak or move forward, or backward, which is where my brain is screaming to go. We have all seen hundreds of bodies across the years of people and former people alike, and we have sadly become accustomed to it. In modest and separate quantities. This looks like a battlefield from one of the wars—it fills the eye and the mind and spills over. Too much.

Irish throws up violently beside me, and the sound and smell makes me do the same, the effluence spattering on the street in front of me and onto my running shoes. *Running*, I think. *Yes, run. Run away as fast as I can.*

But I can't.

It has been a long time since they've all died, and atop the horror of their sheer numbers, they've been picked over, whether by the monsters that have come to inflict the slaughter or carrion eaters since. Everywhere I look, there's death, pain, and mutilation of the human body. I close my eyes, unable to stand it, frozen in place in broad daylight among a silent, unmoving army.

I feel Irish's hand reach for mine, fumbling and then grasping it tightly, almost painfully.

"What happened?" she asks quietly, breaking the silence.

I have no idea. There are a few dozen zombies just as dead and broken as the others, but not a lot of them relative to the humans. A mostly one-sided battle? Mass suicide brought on by hopelessness?

"We have to go," Irish whispers, her voice cracking and sounding very young. "I want to go."

I nod, unsure what I'm feeling since it feels like all possible emotions are there in my head and heart, whirring around in a blender. There are no adequate words for what we're seeing other than it's as much concentrated misery as I could have imagined in my worst dreams. Bodies as far as I can see in all directions, piled atop one another—a carpet of corpses in a grim, unspeaking testament to the decisions of those tasked with protecting us from evil in whatever form it takes.

Angry. Oh, I'm angry to a degree I've never felt before. At the monsters, but more at the man behind the monsters. The fucking colonel and his cronies, trying for a new start and to solve "problems." Genocide is a poor word for what it means, and it's bad enough they have done that, but somehow unsatisfied with killing almost everyone, they created a mindless clean-up crew to catch the remainder. We didn't see the colonel's body back in the field in New York, but we hadn't exactly been granted time to search either, but I want to drive back there and stab him in the face, up to the hilt of the KNIFE. It won't matter if we find him alive or dead either. I want to cut his head off, tie it to the bumper for the thousand-mile drive, and then hold it up like Medusa's so he can see what he's done.

"Please get me out of here," Irish quietly begs.

I gently pull her around to face away, and then give her what she wanted before and needs now, holding her tight in my arms, tucked against my chest. We stand for a long time and weep for them and for us, and then we leave.

# CHAPTER 16

**T**here's nothing we want to tell everyone else, other than to avoid that area on a full stomach. Both Morgan and Eve ask me for more details after seeing how upset we are, and when I refuse, saying I really, *really* don't want to think about it anymore, nor do they want to know beyond it being a mass open-air graveyard, Eve at least seems to take my word for it and lets it go. Morgan has the look in her eye that says she'll go take a peek for herself anyway, and if she chooses to do that, I'm not going to try and stop her. She'll be sorry too.

Irish goes off for a walk on the beach alone, even shooing Amy away from her. Ajax lopes off down the sand behind her, maybe sensing her distress, but leaves her a cushion of space. I stand and watch them go, depression covering me like a too-large cloak, but there's a tiny bit of relief, though the cost has been high. Not relief at finding all the people, but in dodging, however horribly, an awkward situation with Irish. I understand where she's coming from; affection is in thin supply these days, and we probably all need some, but something like what she has in mind could ruin the tenuous and relative simplicity of our lives. I hope the miserable, but timely, interruption puts the subject to bed. I like Irish well enough as a person and all, but I only have eyes and feelings for Eve and don't want to hurt Irish's feelings or do anything that will ruin the closeness and, therefore, security of the group. I can hope it's a closed topic anyway, and if I'm wrong, I'll have to figure out what to say then.

When is all of this going to end? When will it be enough? We've taken so much over the years and need a break. We need something final to tell us we've won, and we sure as hell haven't ever gotten that. Every time it looks like we can take a deep breath, sit back, and have a beer, we're wrong. Adding insult to injury, it also always seems to get worse.

And so, we continue as normal, whatever the fuck that is.

\*\*\*

Amy and Cody are due to take over guard duty on the wall and head off to relieve Bob and Kuniko. We don't know what time it is, other than it's time to be dark and time to be light; the concept of time means a lot less now. You eat when hungry, sleep when tired, and wake up usually when the sun brings the next day to life. We do, however, mind the time for guard duty, setting a four-hour rotation monitored by a manual kitchen timer that stays in the hotel. Whoever's due next will hear the alarm, rewind it, and then go to the wall. We'd tried different lengths of time at first, but everyone agreed after some experimenting that four hours, especially at night, is about the limit for remaining focused.

Cody is happy enough to let Amy drive from the hotel to the wall, which can be terrifying and fun if she gets sidetracked and goes spontaneously off roading, but she's getting better at it quickly. The dwindling late-afternoon sun still burns hotly down at them in the sky, and a thickening breeze that usually warns of an inbound thunderstorm pushes steadily from the east and keeps them company along the way. They meet up with Kuniko and Bob and swap out.

Nothing stirring, which is good. Amy notices Cody watching Kuniko carefully as they walk to the sedan and leave, and she remembers how he kissed Kuniko after the fight. She wishes someone wanted to kiss *her*.

The wall is a good, or bad, place to do some thinking. Nothing to see usually, other than wildlife going about its business, in the air or in the water, though these nighttime shifts are more difficult than others since they have no light, and Amy feels like she's constantly straining to see something, *anything*, and is jumping at shadows all the time. She'll be exhausted when it's time to leave.

No one knows how old they are anymore. Bob was the first to really notice that fact. Amy thinks she's probably fifteen by now, which makes her, like, at least seven or eight years younger than everyone else. Cody always calls her "kid," which makes her batshit—she does, indeed, like cursing now, even when only inside her head—since she can't tell if it's because he can't remember her name or doesn't respect her enough as a peer in the group to use it. He's the closest to her in age and kind of cute in an army-boy kind of way. Muscles all over the place and freckles, too, which she likes.

But she isn't interested in him, not in that way. Aside from calling her "kid," he treats her like one too. Everyone else just acts as if she's their equal, which is cool, so while she doesn't mind looking at Cody, that is as far as it gets. Amy just wishes for someone closer to her age she could talk to about all this stuff, and, well, if some kissing happens, that would be nice.

As if reading her mind, he interrupts her thoughts. "What're you thinking about, kid?"

*Asshole*, she thinks with a little glee at how the word feels in her mind. "Oh, you know, kittens and unicorns, stuff that little girls think about." He's too clueless or selfish to notice the sarcasm. And while she doesn't really care, she asks him a question back since they're going to be together for four hours, and time passes faster when talking. "What about you?"

"Kuniko," he says with a bit of a sigh. "Did you see her on the beach earlier? In that black swimsuit? I wish she'd relax and wear a bikini like the rest of them, but even in a one-piece, oh boy, she is something."

*Part of why she* doesn't *wear a bikini is because of things like you just said, you big dope*, Amy thinks. "Uh-huh, I see." This conversation isn't going to go anywhere, so she tries to shut it down.

No such luck.

"I really like her. I want to just, I don't know, grab her and run off somewhere and ... um," he hesitates, embarrassed at what he was about to say in front of a kid.

"Yeah, whatever."

Amy doesn't like the tone he just used, and being grabbed and running off doesn't seem like something Kuniko would want to do, at least with Cody. Not that there are a lot of choices for her, but she's so quiet and shy that a guy like Cody is definitely not her type. He's noisy and impulsive, not calm. Amy wonders if she should say something to someone. To Kuniko? Hmm, no, maybe it'll upset her a lot. Morgan? That would be one sure way to make him stop, but Morgan kind of scares her. Well, she kind of scares everyone a little, except for her brother. Him? No, feels like it should be one of the women. Eve? Eve is pretty chill, and Amy feels like she can tell Eve anything. Yeah, she'll tell Eve tomorrow. She'll know what to do.

"I'm just lonely in a grown-up way. And she's so pretty and quiet. I can't stop looking at her. You wouldn't understand since you're still a kid."

"Nope, wouldn't understand that at all ... being lonely."

He finally stops talking, and she drifts back into her thoughts, watching the sun fall steadily toward the horizon and lighting the edge of the world with a beautiful ruby-red and orange glow that looks like a huge fire in the distance. Amy's happy they're at the beach now—it's warm, much warmer than New York, and pretty, like the pictures she'd seen on the internet. Growing up in the foster system meant she changed addresses a lot, but they'd all been in Pennsylvania and nowhere near the coast. None of the families she bounced through had been rich enough to take vacations other than to other family members' homes, so this is her first beach trip, and it's everything she dreamed about. The rolling waves that never take time off, building sandcastles, finding neat shells, and learning to swim in the ocean have been really fun for her. All she wants is someone her age, even if a girl, to hang out with and talk to. That and for all the zombies to go away so they can just live here in peace.

***

A couple of hours later, it's a full, deep dark, and they're close to the end of their shift. Cody is drifting to sleep; his head bobbing down and then snatching back up as he fights fatigue. Amy is struggling too—guard duty makes her so nervous about something sneaking up on them that she doesn't usually get tired because her heart is always racing. She'll crash like only a teenager can do when they get back to the hotel, but while here, she feels like she's had an energy drink—her body buzzing and all in a hurry. Tonight, it's super-duper dark and creepy quiet, and while she wrestles to stay alert, it's difficult.

And so, while her attention drifts, she misses the single figure making its way across the span of the bridge, stealthy as a ninja, keeping to the darkest part of the night and moving steadily along the concrete surface. The moon is hidden behind clouds, casting a faint, silvery light around their edges, but there's not enough illumination to throw a shadow behind the male figure. He walks as he has been walking for weeks, on worn-flat sneakers he's had since the end of the old and beginning of the new. A thousand miles on foot on the abandoned highways of the country has nearly rubbed through the remaining soles, but he doesn't notice trivial things like that any longer. No, he's drawn to the wall, to the child's mind, open to him as it had been back then.

She'd told him their plans without meaning to or being able to do anything about it then, and now he and his remaining cadre are here. His followers have dwindled on their own trek south, falling prey to the predators now more abundant than in the past. Wild packs of dogs and wolves have plagued them along the route, picking off those in the back of his herd and making a general nuisance of themselves. Dogs are difficult for zombies to defend against, and canines of all sizes actively seek them out. Too fast to pursue, hard to grab, catch, and eat, and smarter than many of the other remaining animals, they're a constant, nagging presence. They don't eat the zombies they kill, their primal senses tell them not to, but those senses also tell them the abominations that look like their former owners should be scoured from the planet. Dogs don't know the word, but it's karma.

Some of the group had simply drifted to the side of the road, crumpled, and died, out of energy from the lack of food. They had been halved by the journey; still a formidable army, numbering over a thousand but diminished nonetheless. That worries him not at all—human-type concerns don't register in the remnants of his mind. There are others here, many, *many* of them, and he can sense their jumbled thoughts and feel their endless hunger. His army will be reinforced.

He's come alone to connect with the child again, to learn and see. The susurrus of the tide masks any scuff of footsteps, and he stops just outside the barely visible glitter of shattered glass ahead of him, staring at the deep shadows of the barrier blocking the island. He holds still as he had before, taking what he needs from her for a minute or two, and then reverses course back to the mainland. As quiet as before, a creeping wraith of death with a single thought in mind.

**GATHER TO ME**

***

Amy notices the faint whistling sound and thinks Cody is maybe trying to do that to stay awake, which is stupid and annoying. But when she looks across the platform, he's asleep, head down against his chest. There's a tugging inside her skull that feels vaguely familiar, almost like a hook in the center of her head, pulling toward the mainland. She shakes her head, trying to come more awake in the gloom and feels the tug weaken a little. It's uncomfortable, almost like something is in there, roaming around, and she pinches herself on the neck, hard, and it's gone. It leaves her feeling all wiggly inside her head but vanishes as quickly as it had come, just a remaining tickle near her nose. She resists the urge to throw something at Cody to wake him up and just sits looking out at the nothing across the bridge. *Only a little while longer*, she thinks, *before Morgan and her brother are due to relieve us.* She then stands up so she won't drift off. They'll be annoyed with Cody for falling asleep and happy with her for not, so she's pleased at the thought.

She wipes her nose absently across her sleeve, the dark masking the trail of blood that has caused the tickle.

\*\*\*

And off to the east, the wee storm that had started to spin near Africa some weeks back looms less than seventy miles off the South Carolina coast. No longer small, it's a gathering monstrous madhouse spin cycle of moisture, wind, and Nature's wrath, boiling its way toward the Eastern Seaboard with the island smack-dab in the center of its path. Heavy waves push ahead, building walking mountains of water, encouraged by the chasing winds that fly across the ocean with nothing to stop or slow them. It roars deep in its center, dragging ever-more fuel from the water. It leaps across, looking for an outlet and racing for land.

It is, after all, hurricane season.

# CHAPTER 17

The discovery of the field of bodies makes everyone edgy and nervous, especially since we've had a few quiet weeks and have begun to feel secure here in our new sanctuary. Something has killed thousands of people, and of course, we know what that something has to be, which points toward us not being alone on the island after all. The batch we killed earlier had been a large one by our typical standards but not big enough to wipe out all those people on their own. With only the two vehicles—and the wall to mind, now in both directions—we spend the entire next day searching all the roads and neighborhoods, working from a pair of paper maps and allocating sections between cars, and marking those off as we go. Starting just after dawn and continuing until dusk, we find nothing. Unless they're hiding en masse deep in the woods somewhere, we check every possible place that can hold what we figure has to be a corresponding number of zombies; in other words, many hundreds or more without running into anything. No guarantee, of course, but we have been as thorough as we can and feel marginally better by the end of the day.

Rain has accompanied the search, at first a petulant drizzle paired with an increasing breeze from the east. It gets heavier in the afternoon, a steady rain but not the typical summer in-and-out downpour delivered by the near-daily afternoon thunderstorms here. The tide roils along the shore too; Hilton Head is a nice family-friendly beach most of the time, with gentle breakers and limited undertow since the slope of the beach as it meets the ocean is nearly flat and allows you to wade well out into the surf before reaching water at your waist. The sour weather limits our line of sight, and whoever is in the Jeep (mostly me) is drenched since putting the top up will cut visibility even further.

A fruitless day, which leads to a(nother) restless night.

*\*\**

The core of the storm creeps closer, and the zombies scattered beyond the bridge, across on the mainland, gather to their master.

# CHAPTER 18

Amy and I are on the wall that night, taking the second shift that covers the darkest hours leading up until dawn when we'll rotate out. Since the timer is back at the hotel, I have no idea when we're due to be relieved, but my internal clock says sometime fairly soon, and I'm glad for it. Somehow, I've messed up the guard rotation and given her two night shifts in a row, and she's exhausted. I'm worn out from the day, too, but prop myself up with a warm energy drink on the way to the wall. Not my favorite kind of drink for taste—cough medicine with bubbles, to be honest—and warm is even worse, but it does the job and is free, so I take advantage. Amy's restless in the rain, though, constantly fiddling with the minigun Bob has welded to one of the staircases, swinging it back and forth between the stops he's added.

As Bob was doing those, he explained that by putting little blocks of steel to the left and right, the gun will stay trained on the surface of the bridge and not waste ammo into the air far left or right if someone gets carried away when shooting. Like everything else Bob does, this makes good practical sense. Anything approaching the wall will be shredded by the combination of the claymores strung on each side barrier wall for more than fifty yards out, the jagged collection of glass strewn from side to side, and the devastation delivered in hot lead by a gun firing hundreds or thousands of rounds per minute into a tight space. The mines are rigged with trip wires strung from the trucks to the walls we can control by pull strings from the platforms. We've thought about leaving the wires to be triggered by contact but then decide if a single zombie, or a deer wandering off course, trips a bomb, it'll be wasted, so all of them are strung up to the wall for us to pull as needed. We have an awesome array of firepower that should be more than enough to handle any groups of zombies similar to what we've run into in the past.

The weather really blows though. Literally. The rain has increased through the evening to a near-torrential downpour that makes it almost impossible to see beyond the parked trucks at the foot of the wall. Golf umbrellas are free and in plentiful supply, too, and Bob has rigged a series of vertical pipes along the wall that allows us to slide umbrellas into them and provides shade during the day and cover for rain for whoever is on guard. I watch as two of them are lifted by the wind and thrown pinwheeling around down to the ground below us and then up and off over the edge of the bridge to vanish into the darkness. The wind keeps increasing to the point where it roars above and surrounds us, making it almost impossible to be heard.

Debris from the storm blows everywhere, branches from trees hundreds of yards behind us fly past, some landing on the space in front of us, some continuing their flight over the edge of the bridge. We huddle in ponchos, hunker down in indistinct, miserable lumps, trying desperately to keep vigilant and dry at the same time. Every once in a while, it'll go quiet, or quieter, as the storm seems to take an intake of breath, and aside from the patter of rain on the concrete of the bridge, it'll be oddly peaceful for a few seconds. The wan light of dawn is trying to make a reluctant appearance through the dark clouds and waves of rain hovering above the ocean, but it'll be a struggle.

***

Amy hasn't been able to talk to Eve all day while everyone has been split up and hunting, and now with the curtains of rain and nasty wind, she can hardly say anything now either. She's bothered by Cody's fascination with Kuniko and feels like the rest of them need to know, too, so she creeps over.

Raising her voice to be heard over the wind, she shouts, "I need to tell you something!"

I'm in something of a mood, and my first thought is, *Oh c'mon, now what?* But I know it has to be important for Amy to bring it up out here in the miserable weather, so I lean in toward her and tell her to go ahead.

She explains everything, yelling when she needs to compete with Mother Nature's fury. Shit. We've been here before, ladies and gentlemen. Jack with Eve (sort of), Jack with Amelie (almost), Ned with Eve—none of those had turned out well, and I'm angry to maybe have to contend with it again. Kuniko's recent conversation with me regarding Cody comes back, and while we agreed to say nothing then, I resolve to talk to him tomorrow and tell him to settle down and back off. I'll remind him he can go find gallons of lube in the stores around the island and take care of business in private, and any hooking up will be the women's choice, not his. I can't believe we have yet another person we maybe can't trust, and I stew in silence after Amy finishes talking, and the wind settles for a moment.

Except it isn't silent. The wind is pushing mostly in from the east, which is behind us, but no storm is consistent and completely organized. This one is no different and runs in merry circles from time to time. One of those circles blows the sound of crunching glass faintly to my ear, and I freeze in my crouch.

Wind blowing the glass around? Rain running down the sides and maybe picking lighter pieces up for a ride?

Squirrel? Please?

*A shitload of zombies?*

It's like when you're home alone and hear an odd sound in your house—there's a moment where you don't want to move, don't want to go check, sure that whatever it is will go away if you ignore it. It doesn't exist if you don't look. If you did actually look, well, any horror movie handled how that turned out. Always.

Bob has spent many hours at the wall, working his magic to help keep us safe. Aside from the skewers of metal jutting out from the piles of cars, the minigun, and the umbrella pipes, he's also rigged up two posts for large handheld and battery-powered floodlights.

When I was a kid, flashlights were always a fascination for some reason, bringing the dark to life, but of course, their batteries tended to run down quickly. The ensuing decades have brought huge leaps forward, with LED bulbs that are practically tanning lamps hitting the market, capable of stunning brightness and scale. Holding as still as I can, and reaching one hand over to caution Amy to silence and stillness, I reach the other over to fumble up and find the switch on the nearby post.

And this time, I bring the dead to light instead.

Back in New York, when we had been trying to extricate Irish and Cody from their armored prison, a huge pack of zombies lurched from the trees to chase us. At the time, focused on the task of prying the steel door of the carrier open, I hadn't looked up to see how many there were and asked Amy instead.

Her answer then had been, "I think it's all of them."

It had been thousands then, at least, as far as we could tell as we hauled ass. It's hard to count effectively when you're running away in terror.

It's that many again tonight. An endless horde of them faces us, waiting at the edge of the glass fragments, filling the space between the walls of the bridge, perhaps twenty across. That wouldn't have been bad; we can probably handle that many on our own. What is bad are the countless ranks behind them, stretching so far back that the floodlights can't reach their end.

I gasp and gape. They hold their place, a grisly array of the dead, finally a true army in front of us. Most of them look thinner, more worn down and gaunt than before, and their remaining clothes are literal rags barely covering anything. Soaked to the skin, bedraggled hair and clothes clinging to their scrawny, hungry forms.

*How fun! We're going to get to fight mostly naked zombies! But, can you tell me why we're not running right now?*

Good question.

I'm torn between sending Amy back to the hotel to get everyone and hope they'll get back in time to help me make a last stand that we'll maybe win, and hopping off the wall and fleeing with her to the hotel, grabbing everyone and seeing if there's a way we can hide or escape while the horde navigates the wall and walks the miles. Maybe we can hole up in the building until they lose interest. Or I can stay here and try to buy everyone some time to escape somehow, telling Amy to get them so they can all get out. I doubt Morgan will listen to the last option. All of these ideas race through my mind at lightning speed. I don't relish the idea of being alone at all, but my first instinct is to protect Amy and get her away from what's coming. I turn to whisper to her and am interrupted by the quiet sound of the sedan coming up behind us.

Bob and Morgan.

Morgan's driving and hops lightly out and waves, opening her mouth either in greeting or to ask why I have the floods on. I wave her urgently to silence, and she nods. The two of them creep to the wall and tiptoe up the stairs, peering over the edge, shielding their eyes from the rain with their hands.

"My God …" Bob whispers. I don't know what kind of god he's talking about since whoever has delivered this to our doorstep definitely isn't on our side.

"What are they waiting for?" Morgan asks.

"I don't know. They only just showed up a couple minutes ago."

Amy pipes up. "What do we do now? I'm scared shitless," she says as quietly as she can, this time taking no pleasure in cursing.

I look at Morgan. We have no good way off the island. Our barricade and the host of the dead beyond it is the only way out. The other parallel bridge has no stairs or ladder to get over the barrier of crushed cars. While we've found a small handful of rowboats, kayaks, and canoes on the island, the howling wind and waves will capsize any attempt to row across the inland waterway, and no one can swim that far in nasty weather. There's really only the one choice.

Morgan nods, no smile at the prospect of an upcoming fight this time. There's nowhere left to run. "We fight, and we kill them all somehow. Bob, take Amy with you and go back to the hotel and close it up tight. You'll be safe on the upper floors and should have enough food and water for a long time until they lose interest, if … well, if we don't stop them here. Get her out of here," she snarls, though not at Bob. Just getting ready.

He doesn't say anything, just stares out at the zombies for a moment more and then nods and hustles down the stairs with Amy behind him. They drive off, peeling away fast, wipers slashing to defeat the torrential rain. Morgan goes back down the ladder, and heads over to one of the huge fishing coolers we've brought as watertight storage on the ground for our guns and ammunition, and gears up. I watch her stuff grenades into pockets and hoist one of the machine guns up along with a pair of pistols and her Bo. She clambers back up and hands me a pair of grenades to go with my shotgun, other shotgun, the trusty .45s, and my KNIFE. We're in a shitload of trouble no matter how much damage the mines and minigun are going to do.

"So," she says as she arranges her weapons, not looking at me, "here we are, like always. You and me against everyone."

"Morgan, you don't have to stay. Someone should take care of all of them."

She turns to me, forcing a smile now below eyes full of sadness. "I'm not leaving, you know that. I know you're not leaving either. I'm staying, we're fighting, and we're going to win. I mean, we're the good guys, right? The good guys always win … always," she continues with a sniff, and if it weren't for the rain, I think there might have been a tear or two.

I reach over and grab her in a fierce hug, coming to grips with the fact that after all this time, all the battles, and even going back to our childhood, this might be "it," the end of the journey. "I love you," is all I can say. Is all I need to say and probably all she needs to hear.

"Love you too," she replies as she pulls away, holding me at arm's length and staring back at me. "We're going to win."

Sounds a lot like she's trying to convince me, or herself, or both of us.

I'm not sure how that's going to be possible. We're both scared, maybe for the first time, and we turn back to face the monsters at our doorstep, waiting for them to launch the final assault. I force everything out of my head; no regrets, wishes, fears. All of it out. We're going to fight, we're going to kill a lot of them, and we … well, we're going to see what happens when they start moving.

But they don't. They simply stand there beyond the glass. Thousands of hungry eyes stare at us, and in normal circumstances, they would have charged immediately since we're food, but no one moves. We keep watching them, but after five minutes or so of nothing, we look at each other in puzzlement. Something's holding them in place, and I finally realize what it has to be. "An alpha. There is an alpha here keeping them where they are. Why though?"

"No clue. Do we just start shooting and blowing them up? Feels like once this starts, it's not going to stop, but I'm going to admit, I'm not looking forward to that. We wait, I guess?"

She's right. While Morgan has picked her share of fights over the years, and I have always stood by her side (sometimes unhappily), I'm glad for more moments of not being dead.

We all just stand there, watching each other for the first twitch of movement, when I hear the sound of the car behind us.

No.

Everyone piles out of the car, like bitter clowns. Bob, Amy, Irish, Cody, Kuniko, Eve, and the two dogs. Must have been cozy. Wordlessly, they all gather weapons from the ice chests and climb up to join us.

Bob is about to speak with a bit of an apologetic look on his face, but Irish pipes up first. She looks over at me and gives a brave attempt at a smile. "Boss, this one time, no one is going to listen to you. This is everyone's fight, sink or swim." She steps to the minigun, wrapping her hands around the handles.

"That's a lot of fucking zombies," Cody says, gazing over the unmoving mob. "You didn't tell us it was like, a billion of them. Not that it would've changed our minds, but Jesus, look at all of them."

I'm not sure if I'm happy, angry, or sad. Maybe all of those, but we're going to live or die together, and I guess there's some sense to that.

"Why are they waiting?" Kuniko asks.

Morgan explains. We haven't seen an alpha in a long time, not since our flight from the fortress in Kansas when we had rescued Kuniko, Bob, and Maya. Then we talk through strategy, when we'll pull the trip wires for the mines, which side each of us is going to shoot at, when to throw grenades, all of it. We have a lot of ammunition, I know that, but I don't think we have enough for the looming wave, but I decide to keep that to myself.

More waiting, and while we do, the storm lessens. A little. The wind is still gusty, and the rain still drenches us over and over, as if unsatisfied with doing it once, but the

light is increasing steadily until we can see the far reaches of them. Way, way back toward the mainland, probably a quarter of a mile or more of zombies are packed onto the bridge, all tight together.

"I don't like this. Why are they waiting?" Amy says from beneath the hood of her poncho.

I agree. I'm at the point where either it's time to fight, or they should fuck off, but I'm admittedly getting impatient with waiting. The moment I think that, another old saying comes to mind one more time: Be careful what you wish for.

# CHAPTER 19

There's a shuffling in the crowd, and for a moment, I think the attack is beginning and tighten my grip on the shotgun, ready to open up, but they're just moving to the side instead.

One figure moves between them, walking with ease and without urgency toward us. It's a man, somewhere before middle age, with thinning dark hair sweeping straight back above his bare forehead and strong, high cheekbones. He stops before the field of shattered glass begins, and part of me half expects his followers to lie down on the jagged pieces to allow him to walk closer on a former-human footbridge. I can see well enough now that I notice his eyes are solid orbs of black, no color or separation, just blank, ebony, lifeless marbles staring across the space at us.

"What the ..." Cody mutters.

I realize he and Irish have probably never seen an alpha before. Clearly, there had been one coordinating the series of attacks on their base in New York with the feints and flanking maneuver, but in that huge assembly of the dead and the chaos of the battle, they probably wouldn't have picked out the boss. I explain again, very quickly, not taking my eyes off the bridge.

The alpha doesn't take his eyes off us either; in fact, he seems to be looking at us one at a time, pausing, and then moving to the next. I'm on the far left side, so on his far right, and am the last one he turns his implacable and expressionless face toward. And then, he stops. My luck never ends. I'm tempted to take a shot at him right now but have the wrong weapon for it. Shotguns are great for up-close, blow-them-to-smithereens-type work, but these are both loaded with shot versus shells, so they will do no damage at this distance.

*RRRHHEEEEEEE!*

An unbearable noise invades my mind, sudden and shocking. It's like the sound of various night critters here on the island, but amplified, there's a million of them all at once, and someone turns up the volume beyond measure. I double over, hands covering my ears, as if that'll help, trying to escape the invasive screech raking at the inside of my skull. I can't move beyond that; it's so loud that I want to throw up, and vertigo attacks my balance. The sound peaks, wanes for a second, and then slowly subsides to an angry, buzzing undertone.

**KILLER OF BRETHREN**

What? That's inside my head, too, like subtitles on a massive movie screen stretching across everything I can see with my eyes shut, as if *that* makes any sense, amid the rest of the madness of the new world. A stark white background with bold, powerful letters stamped upon it. We have run into plenty of alphas over time, and aside from the one I'd called the "Queen" very early on, interactions have consisted of my killing them as quickly as possible. I'd had some conversations with her, pantomime for her and talking for me, where she insisted "we" get pregnant to provide food for her since babies would have kept her young looking. We disagreed with that, violently, and she's now headless in a North Carolinian cul-de-sac.

**NOT TRUTH**

Is it, he, reading my mind?

**YES**

Oh. I replay what I've just thought about and disagree. I cut off her head myself. And I enjoyed it too. She's very headless and very dead. Truth, motherfucker.

**STOP**

**NOT YOUNG**

**MORE**

He doesn't budge as we "talk," and I guess I'm not moving either since Morgan shoves her way through everyone and pushes against me. "What is going on? Are you all right?"

"Yeah … well, no. That guy can talk inside my head, sort of. And he can read minds too," I say with a wave toward the mob and the alpha.

Everyone stares at me like I've lost my mind.

Finally, Morgan just asks, "Are you shitting me?"

"I wish I was," I answer.

Cody snatches his assault rifle to his shoulder and takes quick aim as he speaks. "Fuck this! I'm taking him down. Let's see how well he reads minds when *his* is splattered all over the rest of them." I watch him try and squeeze the trigger, instantly feel/hear the whining sound vanish to nothing in my head, and then see Cody wince and blink his eyes, his trigger finger frozen in place. "I can't move my hand, and there's this noise … oh, the noise. It hurts!" he moans, letting the rifle's barrel point back toward the ground. The alpha's face is turned to Cody, the dead stare boring into the kid as he groans, close to collapsing.

Then the alpha turns back to me, and Cody gasps in relief. I, on the other hand, am violated once more with the keening, ringing invasion of my mind. It's unbearable, and I "tell" him to cut it down, or we won't be able to have a conversation; not that I really want one, but if I'm going to have to go through this craziness, I want it to be, well, less crazy. The sound subsides enough to be manageable, and we have a little chat.

He tells me everything. What we believed from the conversations with the Queen had been close, but I'd misunderstood her a little. Yes, she wanted us to have babies, and, yes, they were for the zombies. But it wasn't to keep her young, it was to replenish their food supply. Everything is running down—the scathing waves of zombies in the beginning has wiped out huge swathes of the (small to begin with) remaining human population, the scarcity of resources and safety for the survivors is scant, and many more people have died from hunger, exposure, or killing each other. It explains why the ones in New York had corralled the town's few residents into the cooler in the grocery store. They had to ration their food then, and the situation is even more dire now, which is why the alpha, and his troop, have followed us all the way to the beach.

We're to go make babies, as many as we can. Even though there are just the five women here, he tells us they will find other survivors and bring them to us to create a little procreation society for them. We'll be safe on the island as long as we do what we're told. A truce, he offers. Except for the part where we will turn the infants over to them. And the part where we'll be forcing the women—and the men, for that matter—to partake in an abominable act. Have sex, he says. You humans like to have sex.

Bad enough to expect the women to submit to having unwilling intercourse—we've had enough of that, thank you very much. But then they will carry a baby to term, love it with everything they have for nine months, and then give it up to *be fucking eaten by a horde of zombies*. No deal! Survival isn't worth that, none of it. No way am I putting my people through that, and I know they'll agree with me. I'm tired of it, all of it. Running, hiding, fighting, feeling unsafe. We're going to make a stand, no matter how it turns out. We're the good guys after all, like Morgan said, and the good guys always win. Right?

I tell him he can take his offer and stick it up his shriveled zombie ass.

He doesn't like that at all, anger flickering across his face, the first time I've seen any emotion.

**WE ARE MANY**

Yep, you sure are. We have a lot of bullets and the wall. We're taking our chances. And if you kill all of us, there's nothing to eat. Put that in your pipe and smoke it.

## A LESSON

Our connection ceases abruptly, and Amy gives a surprised yelp, flinching back from the edge of the wall, blood pouring from her nose and ears in a shocking red torrent that matches the blaze of the sun now emerging fully above the horizon. The poor kid collapses, screaming in pain and flailing around as Eve rushes to her side, trying to comfort her and staunch the flood. Everyone else gasps in shock, and for once, the voice inside is welcome and smart.

*Hey, I just noticed something. His connection seems like it's only good for one at a time. You, then Cody only when he drew down on him, back to you, now Amy. I'm thinking he can only do one, and also, if he switches over to control his little army, he probably can't do anything to you and yours. Besides, you got any better ideas?*

I don't, and just as the ringing starts again, I look at Morgan and nod my head toward him before he gets all the way in. She smiles, the way she always does, even though it's still a grim one.

And fires her rifle.

And misses him, taking down the zombie just behind and over his shoulder, splattering its head into a fine mist of goo and blood.

The connection is severed instantly, and I regain full control. I fire at the alpha with my shotgun, but the pellets disperse before reaching him, and he ducks back into the crowd, letting their bodies swallow and shield him. We've unfortunately seen that trick before. Everyone else gets the hint and opens up.

And the final battle begins.

# CHAPTER 20

*Muuuuuuhhhhh!*

We've heard that cry so many times over the years, usually only from a few dozen mouths at most. This is a wave of sound that dwarfs anything we've heard before, even eclipsing the waning sounds of the hurricane still howling its fury over the top of us, a wave of noise that spills across our defenses. And then the wave of monsters comes, suddenly and all at once, flying at the wall in their shuffling quick jog, though faster than ever, as if sensing the stakes are higher this time. The first rank staggers onto the glass field, not slowing as the shards bite into their mostly bare feet, edging toward the makeshift barricade of the trucks.

Irish opens up with the minigun. If the roar of the storm and the cry of the zombies is loud, this is a monstrous riot of thunder that overtakes all other sound. It's awesome and terrible at the same time—the gun spews a rampage of bullets into and through the leading pack, carving through them in a gruesome reaper's scythe of death. Zombies are softer than regular people, and the bullets go through Zombie One to hit Zombie Two behind it before *thudding* with finality into the third one deep. Irish is taking an incredible toll on them as they keep coming, holding them from getting any closer as we all join in, picking at the edges while she steadily sweeps the gun from side to side, methodically building a carpet of corpses on the glass.

"Cody, the mines!" I shout over the racket, wanting him to add the claymores' destructive flurry of explosive and flying shards of metal to the fray, knowing they'll obliterate the flanks and funnel the center of their mass right into Irish's sights.

He jumps to where the strings are all gathered, marked by colored tape for which is which section, and pulls the blue lines and looks out with a victorious grin. Nothing. He yanks the cords again. Same result. He finds and pulls red, then green, then silver. No booms, no hail of metal to cut them to shreds.

Uh-oh.

Everyone is screaming their own version of a battle cry as we lay waste to the zombies drawing closer to the foot of the wall. Even Eve has let Amy go, knowing there's nothing to be done for the girl if we die, and is firing a big pistol into the crowd in front of us. A handful of tears leak down her face as she does so, and it hurts my heart for her a little bit, finally having to fully submit to the new order of things. But as Morgan had told her once, it's time to fight or die. There's nothing in between.

We aren't getting all of them. Without the destruction from the mines, some of the runners are reaching the wall.

Irish's weapon does the most damage, holding the bulk of them from making more than incremental progress, though they're creeping ever closer, leaving a massive pile of dead zombies for those trailing behind to clamber over. But that also guards those following ranks from the guns and reduces their casualties. We need the mines, but while Cody is intermittently trying to pull the cords over and over, the result is the same: nothing.

"The lines are cut out there, I can see it!" he shouts.

There's nothing to be done about that. The strings are a dozen yards away from the foot of the wall, out in the middle of the clambering horde coming for dinner.

Instead of trying to climb the jagged spikes of the wall, the leading monsters simply throw their bodies against them, impaling themselves with the sound of a butcher's cleaver hitting home.

*Thunk-thump, thunk-thump, thunk.*

As more and more dodge our fire and reach the metal spears, I realize what they're doing—filling them up and creating a writhing ramp of the mostly dead for the following ones to use. They're going to climb a grisly buttress of their fellows to reach us. The alpha isn't able to use any of the tactics he used against the army back in the North, feints and flanking moves, but it's a strategy nonetheless. Unlimited "bullets" means you can waste a few.

We're losing.

And there are still hundreds and hundreds of them.

"I'm almost out!" Irish screams from the other platform.

I glance over at the minigun's base, seeing it piled with a gleaming carpet of spent shells, spitting ever more of them from the discharge and watch the ammo belt being consumed oh-so rapidly. We don't have unlimited bullets, and we're going to die in less than a minute after Irish runs out of ammo. The other guns can't possibly hold off the wave of the scampering monsters now thickening in the spaces between the trucks. I'm about to tell everyone to get off the wall, run, climb into the vehicles, and just go find a place to hide, when impulse strikes.

But not mine.

Cody and Morgan make the same decision in the same instant. I watch, frozen in shock, as first he and then my sister jump off the wall and toward the oncoming zombies and understand what they're going to do. If they can pull the trip wires, it'll destroy the attackers, or near to it. But it'll also be suicide—the ends of the cords to detonate the mines are well within the cone of destruction that's going to erupt, and they'll be caught in it too. The wall is over ten feet high, and they have to jump well out to avoid the spikes.

Somehow, Cody lands cleanly, finding a tiny space between bodies, and dashes off toward the nearest strings to the mines, slashing away with his own knife against the leering batch that diverts instantly away from their assault on the wall to pursue him.

Morgan isn't so lucky, maybe for the first time in her life. She has almost landed when one of the spike-impaled zombies reaches a hand toward her falling body and catches just enough of one foot to unbalance her in midair. She lands awkwardly and with a cry, tumbles once and lies on the ground holding her ankle, looking desperately at Cody's racing form. He runs through their arms, faster than we'd seen him on the beach, dodging the hands and lunging mouths that seek to stop him, and then dives for the group of dangling cords.

Shit, my sister is down there!

I jump too. Morgan is hurt and exposed, and without hesitation, I leap out over a pair of zombies just reaching the top of the wall, leaving them to be killed by Eve or whoever else. I'm not leaving my sister alone, not now, not ever. Just as I land and reach her, diving to cover her body with mine, the world takes in a deep, silent breath …

… And then lets it out in a stunning concussion of light, noise, and destruction.

The surface of the bridge lurches in protest against the high explosives that are unleashed across its surface, shredding hundreds of the zombies in the cross fire path of the whirling hail of steel shards. Just before I close my eyes and hug tight to Morgan, I look at Cody and see him obliterated in an instant. I feel a few pieces of hot shrapnel rain down harshly against my back and wince but am otherwise unharmed. We're so close to the wall, we've been spared.

My ears ring again, this time on the outside. It feels like I have mammoth pillows against the sides of my head, and I'm disoriented until Morgan pushes against me, shouting at me to get off and up.

Everything in front of me, back toward the mainland, is destroyed. The trucks are perforated in hundreds of places, the concrete is scarred and blackened everywhere a mine has been mounted, and zombie bits and pieces are scattered in all directions, leaving few whole ones lying prone and even fewer standing. Cody's sacrifice has cost our enemy almost everything.

I stand up, unsteadily, digging a .45 out from its place at my waist and firing at the enclosing few until I hear the *click*. Empty. My other pistol is lost somewhere. My companions also click on empty as they pick off the residual climbers, all our ammunition gone, and if there's any killing left to be done, it's going to be the old-fashioned way, by hand. With Morgan down. I have the KNIFE, but that's it.

It's quiet now. The fight has raged for probably no more than ten minutes, maybe less, but in that time, the wind has settled to a persistent breeze but nothing more. Some of the near corpses are making weak mewling attempts at their battle cry, but none crawl toward me. It seems Cody has gotten them all.

Except, of course, he hasn't. Our luck is never that good.

The pile of bodies Irish has created with the minigun wiggles at the top, a head appearing over the edge as the alpha ascends and reaches the pinnacle of his own gruesome wall. He stands staring at us as a dozen or more zombies join his flanks and wait. We aren't going to be able to kill all of them, not with our mostly bare hands, so it's time to run.

I reach down and hoist Morgan up off the ground. She curses in pain and hops on her one good foot to the base of

the wall, and I help her up to the reaching arms of Bob, to safety, just as I hear a noise behind me and turn around.

He's there, standing still just a few paces away. Just him. His vastly diminished army is well behind him and unmoving.

So this is how it's going to be. An old-fashioned fight indeed.

I'm exhausted, running on reserves of adrenaline only, and feel a welcome flood of it as I bring out my KNIFE. Inches of gleaming steel honed to a razor's edge during hours of boredom and readiness.

*All the better to cut your head off with, my dear.*

That's about right.

I lunge with the shining blade, intending to do just that, but he's fast. Horribly fast, faster than me, and he catches my arm at the wrist. His grip is incredible, a vise closing down implacably on my wrist, crushing it until I can't hold the blade any longer and drop it with a clatter onto the bridge. I'm much larger than he is, at least thirty or forty pounds heavier, but he's miserably strong, far stronger than he should be.

Ragged teeth grin in triumph as he pulls my arm down and tries to lean in toward my neck. I press my other arm between us and shove back with every desperate ounce of strength I possess, but he's too powerful and forces me backward, toward the edge of our wall.

Toward an unoccupied spike on the outside edge, all three feet of its jagged surface ready and waiting to puncture me.

He forces me back, back, back. I try to plant my feet but to no avail. I take a chance and kick him in the zombie balls, and he doesn't even flinch. He grips my arms and keeps shoving me relentlessly, and I hope someone up there has a bullet left. For me or him, either one.

Finally, he stops. My back is a scant few feet from the reaching blade of the spike, and I feel myself trying to arch my back and avoid it.

**OVER**

I feel his grip tighten for the final push, and then I do the one thing he doesn't expect. I relax and give no resistance and spin halfway around as he lunges forward, now out of control as he used all his strength in that last shove, holding tight to his arms, whirling him around, too, and slamming him onto the spike instead, back first. Zombie bodies are a little softer after all, and the steel juts a foot through his chest as he loses his grip on me.

**NO!**

Yes!

A spear in the torso isn't going to kill him—we've seen many of them survive far worse injuries and keep moving. Tired now beyond anything I've ever experienced, I walk slowly over to where I've dropped my KNIFE and pick it back up. I'm going to kill him and then deal with his followers as best as I can, to try and buy my people a few minutes' worth of a head start. Cody gave himself up for us; I can do the same.

His eyes are dimming when I get back but still flare with a horrible deep-black anger. The invasive ring flutters weakly inside my mind, but I push back, and it vanishes. I mean to cut his head off, but then I decide I'll feel better with something a little different.

Raising the KNIFE over my head, I ram every inch of it into his skull, hilt deep in his left eye. Shock on his face and then nothing.

He's finally dead.

And now for the rest. With no gun, no bullets, and my KNIFE embedded in his head, not that it would have done me much good against the dozen-plus remaining monsters. I turn to face them, resigned to what's next but trying to summon enough anger to make them work for it. They stand atop their wall, gazing down, lit in the morning sun's rays, and then as one, they simply turn and leave.

# CHAPTER 21

s badly as I want to just collapse where I am, I climb the wall of bodies and watch what remains of the horde meander off, more aimlessly than when they arrived, and I realize without their leader controlling and directing them, they're back to being a mindless pack. They move along the bridge, and I stay there until they fall out of sight.

We won. Somehow, we won.

*Not somehow. That impulsive kid you were going to have to talk to gave his life for yours, all of you. He doesn't jump and pull the detonator cords, you're all dead. You misjudged again, a little anyway, and you were wrong again, but for once, it turned out to the good. Nice move on the zombie, I'll give you that.*

We're all shell-shocked and stunned to some degree, maybe by the fact that we're still alive. I stand at the base of the wall and look up at the faces smudged by gunpowder, dirt, rain, and blood. They look back and then reach down to help me back up onto our side of things. Ajax comes over and nudges my hand, probably pissed he'd been left out of a fight for once, or maybe just making sure I'm okay.

I am. Tired as shit, relieved, but okay.

No one says anything. Eve and Kuniko stare at me, distraught and maybe a little angry at me for also going over the wall. Despite their previous warnings about me doing things like that, there was no choice. This was really it—kill or be killed, go big or go home, all those trite phrases. Bob keeps watching the retreating squad of zombies, unmoving as if he's unable to believe they're actually leaving and thinks if he takes his eyes off them, they'll come storming back. Irish still has her hands on the grips of the minigun, even though it's empty, just looking over the battlefield and breathtaking destruction strewn in front of the wall. Her face is covered with tears, and I realize just how close we've come to losing everything and everybody. Morgan and Amy are on the platform with Amy's head resting on Morgan's lap, conscious and apparently okay enough. And maybe that's the right words for it now: okay enough.

After a few moments, we all just wordlessly climb down the stairs, pile into the vehicles, and go back to the hotel. We don't leave anyone at the wall. We don't need to.

***

Everyone walks down to the beach. Like most storms, the one that had hit us drags fine weather behind it, and the day is warm and clear without the typical humidity. I keep going when I reach the water, going fully clothed out into the surf, letting the still-tall waves wash over and scour the battle's residue from me. I sense rather than see the rest follow me into the ocean and simply stand there, seeking the peace that its steady, unending motion will bring, a reminder that some things never, and yet always, change. Watching the undulating surface, I say a small thanks to Cody.

I flinch at first when a soft hand touches my arm. It's Eve, smiling gently at me but with a bit of a hesitant look in her eyes. She's checking to see if I'm okay, too, and I am, it just feels like I'm letting go of it all. Years of constant fear and tension, running, hiding, and fighting for survival. All of it. I gradually smile back and then take her in my arms. I'm going to kiss her; not right this second but soon. And we're going to hold hands and walk on the beach. And get old together. And maybe other stuff.

I can't stop smiling.

We won.

That means we're the good guys.

# AUTHOR'S NOTE

I f you're reading this, it means a couple of things. One, you've been along for the entire ride, which is good, and for that, I say, "Thank you." Two, it means I did enough right to keep you reading, which is also good. These characters and stories have been running around in my head and out of my fingers for over ten years now, and I have enjoyed their trip and, in a way, feel privileged to tell their story. I hope you've enjoyed it all too.

I originally thought I was going to write something of an epilogue here, where I'd go into short paragraphs about what happened to everyone since I dig that in the movies and thought readers might too. But that would imply the series was over. I thought it might be over after *One* and was wrong. *Sanctuary* also felt like the last when I finished it, but I left enough bread crumbs along the way for you (and me) that things began to come together, and here we are.

I don't know what will happen next; I kind of never do. I'm the steward of the tales that come along, and there were lots of times I have been as surprised as (hopefully) you were. If I was going to leave off anywhere aside from thank you again, it's that I will keep watching the wall.

And we'll see if anything creeps over the edge.

Greg Rode, 2022

P.S.—For anyone curious, the important book was *The Fountainhead*.

# ABOUT THE AUTHOR

GREG RODE

**GREG RODE** is the author of the *Sanctuary Chronicles* series. He lives in Cornelius, North Carolina, with his family and two small dogs that aren't nearly as tough as Ajax and Jack.

The cabins and lake described in the novels are real and have been in the family for well over a century. It would indeed be a superb place to go for sanctuary, but there's not enough room for everybody, which is why he doesn't say where it is exactly. That and his grandmother once said not to say where it was if he ever wrote a book there. Since it was very unwise to mess with Grammie, you're on your own when the zombies come.

He is currently working on an epilogue and prequel to the series, though not always at the same time.